I Wonder Why

Flutes Have Holes

and Other Questions About Music

Josephine Paker

Kingfisher

NEW YORK

KINGFISHER
Larousse Kingfisher Chambers Inc.
95 Madison Avenue
New York, New York 10016

First American edition 1995
10 9 8 7 6 5 4 3 2 1 (HB)
10 9 8 7 6 5 4 3 2 1 (RLB)
LIBRARY OF CONGRESS CATALOGING-IN-PUBLICATION DATA
Paker, Josephine.
    I wonder why flutes have holes and other questions about
    music/by Josephine Paker.
    1st American ed.
        p.   cm.
    Includes index.
    1. Music — Miscellanea — Juvenile literature.
    [1. Music — Miscellanea. 2. Questions and answers.]
    I. Title. II. Series: I wonder why (New York, N.Y.)
    ML3928. P35 1995 94-45002 CIP AC MN

ISBN 1-85697-583-5 (HB)
ISBN 1-85697-640-8 (RLB)
Printed in Italy

Series editor: Clare Oliver
Series designer: David West Children's Books
Consultant: Peter Thoms
Thanks to: Waseda University, Tokyo
Illustrations: Peter Dennis (Linda Rogers); Diane Fawcett
    (Artist Partners); Chris Forsey; Nick Harris (Virgil
    Pomfret); Biz Hull (Artist Partners) cover;
    Tony Kenyon (B.L. Kearley) all cartoons; Nicki Palin;
    Richard Ward; David Wright
    (Kathy Jakeman).

CONTENTS

How do you sing a round?

A round is a song for two or more singers. Everyone sings the same tune, but they start singing at different times. When the first singer finishes the first line, the second singer starts, and so on. One of the best-known rounds is called *Frère Jacques.*

● A round gets louder and louder as each singer joins in, and softer and softer as everyone finishes their part.

6 × 7 = 42

● Singing can help you to learn things—your multiplication tables, for instance. Singing makes them much easier to remember.

● People sing *Happy Birthday to You* more than any other song in the world. At first it wasn't a birthday song at all. It was called *Good Morning to All.*

● An opera is a musical play in which every single word is sung— even something as ordinary as "May I come in, please?"

Who sings in the bath?

Just about everyone loves to sing in the bath. Your voice is your own special musical instrument, which you can "play" any-time you like. As you sing, air wobbles across stretchy ribbons in your throat, known as vocal cords. We hear this vibrating air as sound.

● Voices sound beautiful in the bath. The sounds bounce off the walls and the water to make rich, loud echoes.

How do marching bands keep time?

Left, right, left, right! As a band marches along, the players move their feet in time to the music. The big bass drum booms out the beat to keep the band in step.

● The majorette leads the parade. She has a stick, called a baton, which she twirls and tosses high in the air as she marches along.

How fast is fast?

So you know how fast a piece of music should be, the composer tells you how many beats it has in every minute. To copy this speed, you use a metronome. Just set this machine ticking and play in time with its ticks.

• When you listen to music, it's often hard not to join in! Your toes tap and your hands clap to the music's rhythmic beat.

• Your heart beats about 90 times every minute, but you may find it speeds up when you're listening to fast, exciting music.

• Have you heard the song 1,000 ? It has 1,000 beats every minute. It's so fast that you can't hear separate notes —they all smudge together!

Who worked to the beat?

Oarsmen on Greek warships worked in time to the music of a drummer or piper. The beat kept the oars moving smoothly together through the water.

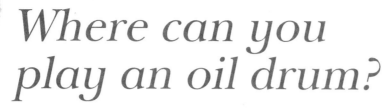

Where can you play an oil drum?

In the Caribbean islands, large empty oil drums are made into musical drums called steel drums. The top is hammered into a curved dish-shape. This metal dish is then beaten and "tuned" until the different parts of the steel drum make a number of musical sounds. Some drums can play 30 different notes.

● Steel bands play outside in the streets or on the beach at carnival time.

Who bangs on the bongos?

A drummer in a South American dance band often plays the bongos. He grips the drums between his knees and taps them with his fingers and the palm of his hand. This makes zippy rhythms that soon get you dancing.

Can drums talk?

In Nigeria, talking drums can even tell the news. The kalangu drum's beats are like a secret language that only a few people are able to understand. The drummer tightens or loosens the drum skin to change the sounds.

● The Tinguian people of the Philippines thought that the sound of thunder was the god Kadaklan, pounding on his drum.

● A lion-roar drum sounds rather like a real lion—scary! You don't beat this drum. Instead you pull a stick or strip of leather through a hole in the top, and a growling noise rumbles out.

9

Where can you find a gamelan?

A gamelan is a kind of orchestra from Indonesia. Drums, gongs, xylophones, and chimes all play together to make a magical tinkling sound. There can be as many as 40 instruments in a gamelan.

● Washboards are just trays to scrub clothes on. But some jazz musicians play them like an instrument. They scrape a stick or thimble across the ridges.

● Gamelan players treat their instruments with great respect.

Are rattles just for babies?

Babies aren't the only ones who like the dry, swishing sound rattles make. The first ones were probably dried plant pods, full of seeds. South American rattles called maracas are still often filled with dried beans. You could fill a yogurt tub with some to make your own rattle.

● The triangle is one of the smallest instruments. Larger triangles are used to warn people about fire in some parts of the world, but sirens work better on noisy roads!

What roars like a bull?

The bull-roarer doesn't really roar like an angry bull! It's a block of wood fixed to a piece of string. You whirl it above your head and it makes a strange screaming noise.

11

Are guitar strings really made of string?

Like all musical strings, guitar strings are usually made of metal or nylon, not string! As you pluck them, the strings shake. This makes the air shake too and we hear it as sound. It rolls around inside the hollow guitar, and makes rich notes.

- You tune a stringed instrument by turning the pegs at the end of its neck. Tightening a string makes a higher note. Loosening it makes a lower one.

- Stringed instruments come in all shapes and sizes. This old lute was made using the hard skin of an armadillo!

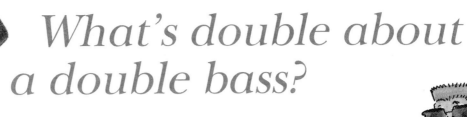

What's double about a double bass?

The double bass got its name because it used to "double," or copy, the cello. "Bass" means low, and the double bass *does* have a deep voice! Pluck one of its thick strings and it makes a very low note.

● Niccolo Paganini was a genius on the violin. He could play it behind his back, upside-down, and with a blindfold on!

How do you learn the sitar?

The sitar (**sit**-ar) is one of the most difficult stringed instruments to play. To learn it, you have to watch and listen to a skilled player. Players learn groups of notes called ragas, and then put them together to make beautiful, haunting music.

● The Indian vina balances comfortably on the shoulder as the player plucks the strings.

13

Why do flutes have holes?

To play the flute, you blow over the blowhole. The air shakes its way down the tube and you hear it come out as a musical sound. You change notes by covering and uncovering the different holes in the flute with your fingers.

● Pennywhistles belong to the same family of musical instruments as flutes—the woodwind family. You play the pennywhistle like a recorder, by blowing into the mouthpiece, and covering the holes.

● Panpipes are named after an ancient Greek god called Pan, who was half goat. He cut some reeds of different lengths, tied them together, and blew across the top.

When is a serpent not a serpent?

When it's a woodwind instrument! It's easy to see how the serpent got its snaky name—it's so curly! It was invented 400 years ago, but isn't played much these days.

● Snakes are deaf, but they sway in time to a snake-charmer's music. They keep their eyes on the pipe, in case it's an enemy snake!

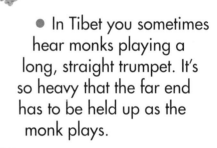

● In Tibet you sometimes hear monks playing a long, straight trumpet. It's so heavy that the far end has to be held up as the monk plays.

How do you stretch brass?

The trombone is one brass instrument that needs stretching. It has a long, sliding arm. The trombonist moves this slide in and out to make the different notes.

Who sits where in an orchestra?

The players in an orchestra all have their own place to sit. This depends on which instrument they play, and which "family" the instrument belongs to. Violins, cellos, and other stringed instruments all sit together at the front and the noisier brass and woodwind instruments are at the back.

● Johann Strauss conducted a vast orchestra in 1872. There were nearly 1,000 players, with over 400 people playing the violin.

● The French composer Jean-Baptiste Lully used to conduct by banging a big stick on the floor. One day, he missed and banged his own foot instead! Ouch!

Drums

French horns

Piano

Harp

Clarinets

Percussion

Trombones

Tuba

Trumpets

Bassoon

Double basses

Flutes

Oboes

Cellos

Violins

● The conductor is the boss. He or she tells the musicians when to play, how loudly to play, how fast, and—of course—when to stop!

Who writes music?

People who write music are called composers. They write down musical notes just as you write down words. Music isn't always written down though. Some people learn how to play a piece of music by simply copying a teacher or something they have heard.

● Many composers don't write down their ideas on paper anymore. They key in the notes on a computer and can immediately play back what they have written.

Which five-year-old composed music?

Wolfgang Amadeus Mozart was a musical genius. At five, he composed his very first piece of music. By the time he died, aged only thirty-five, he had written more than 600 works.

● Mozart was one of the greatest—and youngest—composers. His father took him on a tour of Europe to show him off.

Which composer was deaf?

The German composer Ludwig van Beethoven slowly became deaf. At first he used a curly ear trumpet to help him to hear, but it was no use. Soon he was composing music in his head that he was never able to hear.

● Musical notes are written on a set of five lines called a stave. A high note is written high up on the stave. The shape of the note, and whether it's black or white, shows how long it should last.

● Music isn't always written down. Jazz musicians often make up the music as they go along. This is called "improvisation."

Which is the biggest instrument?

The organ is the biggest musical instrument. Organ music can make the windows rattle! The largest and loudest organ in the world is in Atlantic City, New Jersey. It's so huge that it sounds as loud as 25 brass bands playing together! It has 12 keyboards and over 33,000 pipes. Sadly, this record-breaking instrument doesn't work very well these days.

● The Russian composer Sergei Rachmaninov had enormous hands. Each hand could stretch over 12 keys on the piano—that's probably twice as far as you could manage.

What's the longest piece of music ever played?

It takes all day and half the night to listen to a performance of Erik Satie's *Vexations*. This is because the piece has to be played 840 times. It needs six pianists to take turns with the playing. Just one might fall asleep!

● This enormous guitar in Bristol, England, is so huge that you can climb inside it. If you twang its strings the noise is deafening!

Which is the most valuable instrument?

Three hundred years ago, an Italian called Antonio Stradivari made the most wonderful violins. His instruments are now so rare and so valuable that they cost a fortune— far more than the price of a house!

Who tells stories by dancing?

Ballet is a way of telling a story through music and dance. The sound of the music and the movements of the dancers tell you what's going on as clearly as any story in a book. And, of course, it's beautiful to watch and to hear.

● Sometimes a story is turned into a ballet—*The Tales of Beatrix Potter*, for instance.

● Some street performers are more like gymnasts than dancers—they do daring handstands, somersaults, and leaps!

What's the dance of the spider?

An Italian dance, called the tarantella, is named after the tarantula spider. People used to think that if someone was bitten by this deadly spider, they would only be cured by dancing the wild dance of the tarantella. As the dancer twisted and leaped, all of the onlookers beat time with tambourines and castanets.

● The lowest a limbo dancer has ever limboed is under a flaming wooden bar just 4 inches off the ground. That's less than half the height of this book!

● When you dance the conga, you hold the person in front by the waist and dance along in a line. The longest conga ever stretched the length of 500 ice rinks and was made up of 120,000 people.

Whose singing wrecked ships?

In fairy tales, mermaids were magical creatures—half women and half fish—who lived in the sea near dangerous, rocky coasts. They sang so sweetly that any sailors who heard them forgot everything else—including how to steer their ship.

• In Greek mythology, Orpheus played his lyre so beautifully he persuaded the god of the underworld to free his wife, Eurydice (yoo-rid-i-see). But he broke a promise not to look back at her as she followed him, and lost her after all.

● Saint Cecilia is the patron saint of music. In pictures, she usually has a miniature organ on her lap.

● In a tale by Hans Christian Andersen, a Chinese emperor loved to listen to a nightingale's song. When the bird flew away, the emperor missed it's music so much he had a mechanical model made in it's place

Who played a magic pipe?

In the story of the Pied Piper, a man with a magic pipe enchants the children of Hamelin in Germany. When he plays, they follow him out of town —never to return.

Which frog sings?

Male frogs love to sing. They puff out their throats to make a big space where the air can vibrate and the concert begins. Frogs sing surprisingly loudly, but it's not everyone's idea of music!

• The composer Domenico Scarlatti wrote a piece that is nicknamed *Cat's Fugue*. Scarlatti said that his cat made up the tune as it tiptoed along the keys of his harpsichord!

Which mouse is musical?

The male grasshopper mouse of North America uses his shrill, chirping song to attract a mate. He stands up on his back legs and sings his heart out. It's his way of telling all the female mice around what a fine, strong mouse he is.

Who sings the dawn chorus?

As the Sun rises on spring and summer mornings, the birds wake up and start to twitter. This makes a beautiful dawn chorus. Some songs warn other birds to keep away. Some tell a mate where to find some tasty food.

● Each bird has its own special song, unlike any other's. Birds recognize each other by their song, just as we recognize a friend by their voice.

Who sings under water?

Humpback whales seem to sing to each other under the ocean. Some scientists think the whales are singing about where they've swum and what they've been doing. No other animal's song lasts as long as the humpback whale's, and it can be heard hundreds of miles away.

● Elephants sometimes use their trunks like a musical instrument. They blow through them and make a tremendous trumpeting noise.

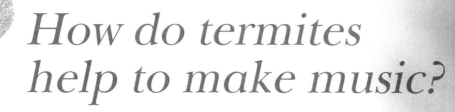

How do termites help to make music?

The didgeridoo (dij-uh-ree-**doo**) is a long musical pipe from Australia made from a log of the eucalyptus tree, which is buried inside a termites' mound. The termites gnaw away at the soft wood inside the log, leaving a hollow pipe. Then the pipe is decorated. Didgeridoos can be hollowed out by hand, but they don't give the same rich sound.

Which harp fits inside your mouth?

The tiny Jew's harp doesn't look like its larger cousin. You put it between your teeth, and twang its metal tongue with your finger. It makes your lips feel funny because the metal vibrates so much.

● Didgeridoo-players can breathe in at the same time as they're blowing out through their instrument.

● The Masai people of Kenya play an instrument called a thumb piano. It has metal strips which you pluck with your thumb.

Which instrument is made with a spiderweb?

Take a cow's horn, make a little hole at the pointed end, cover the wide end with a tough kind of spiderweb, and you have a mirliton (**mur**-lee-ton). These are played in Africa. They make a buzzy sound when you blow or sing through them.

● A jazz musician called Roland Kirk could play three saxophones at once! He must have had big lungs!

● Not all bagpipes come from Scotland. This African goatskin bagpipe has been decorated with a carved wooden goat's head!

Can a robot play the piano?

A clever Japanese robot called WABOT-2 can whizz its fingers over a keyboard much faster than a human can. It can either read new music, or choose a song it has played before and stored in its memory. The cleverest thing about WABOT-2 is its sensitive fingers. It can play gently or furiously.

● WABOT-2's head is like a camcorder. As the robot reads music, the camera "films" what it sees and stores it in its memory to play again.

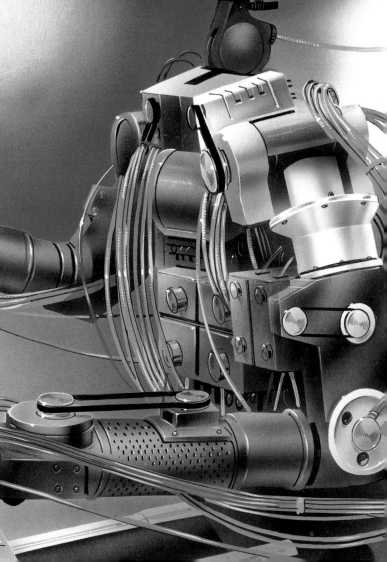

30

Where do people mix music?

In a recording studio, the voices and instruments are recorded separately. The producer mixes the parts together on a machine called a mixing desk. He or she checks the sounds are balanced and every part can be heard clearly.

● Drum machines make the sound of all kinds of drums—but they're only as big as a candy box. Some of them have pads to tap out the rhythm on.

● You can record any sound you like on a sampler —even a dog's bark. You put the sounds you've sampled into tunes as if they were musical notes.

Can you be an entire orchestra?

Synthesizers are machines that can make the sound of every instrument in the orchestra. One minute they sound like a flute, the next they sound like a violin. They'll even play a simple drum pattern to give your music a beat.

Index

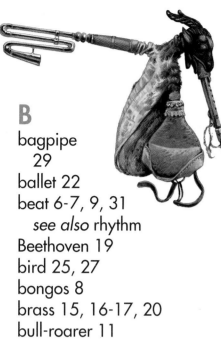

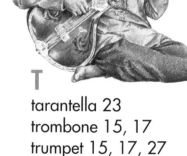

Ex Libris

Philip Conyers

as of 3/85
Ex Libris
Daniel Schmidt

1968

Watteau

Anita Brookner

Watteau

The Colour Library of Art
Paul Hamlyn

Acknowledgments

The paintings and graphic works in this volume are reproduced by kind permission of the following museums, galleries and collections to which they belong: Trustees of the British Museum, London (Plates 28, 32); Cailleux Collection, Paris (Plates, 2, 3); Trustees of the Chatsworth Settlement, Bakewell (Figure 5); City of York Art Gallery (Plate 7); Governors of Dulwich College, London (Plate 20); École Nationale Supérieure des Beaux-Arts, Paris (Plate 6); Marquis de Ganay Collection, Paris (Plate 25); Heugel Collection, Paris (Plate 9); Kunstverzamelingen, Teylers Stichting, Haarlem (Plate 14); Metropolitan Museum of Art, New York - Jules S. Bache Collection, 1949 (Plate 45); Metropolitan Museum of Art, New York - Munsey Fund, 1934 (Plate 37); Musée des Arts Décoratifs, Paris (Plate 4); Musée des Beaux-Arts, Lille (Plate 36); Musée Condé Chantilly (Plate 12, Figure 1); Musée du Louvre, Paris (Plates 13, 16, 17, 24, 26, 27, 30, 34, 43, 47, Figures 2, 3, 4, 6); Musée du Petit Palais, Paris (Plate 5); Museum of Fine Arts, Boston (Plate 10); National Gallery of Art, Washington D.C., Samuel H. Kress Collection (Plates 11, 46); Trustees of the National Gallery, London (Plate 19); National Galleries of Scotland, Edinburgh (Plate 35); Nationalmuseum, Stockholm (Plate 1, Figure 7); Rijksmuseum, Amsterdam (Plate 18); Sir John Soane's Museum, London (Plate 8); Stiftung Preussischer Kulturbesitz, Staatliche Museen, Gemäldegalerie, Berlin-Dahlem (Plates 22, 23, 29, 33, 44); Verwaltung der Staatlichen Schlösser und Gärten, Berlin-Charlottenburg (Plate 33); Trustees of the Wallace Collection, London (Plates 15, 21, 31, 38, 39, 40, 41, 42).
The following photographs were supplied by J. E. Bulloz, Paris (Plate 5); Gilchrist Photo Service, Leeds (Plate 7); Photographie Giraudon, Paris (Plates 6, 25, 36); Michael Holford, London (Plates 2, 3, 8, 9, 15, 19, 21, 31, 38, 39, 40, 41, 42); Rapho Agence Photographique, Paris (Plates 26, 27); Tom Scott, Edinburgh (Plate 35); André Held-Joseph P. Ziolo, Paris (Plates 12, 13, 16, 17, 24, 30, 34, 43, 47).

Published by the Hamlyn Publishing Group Ltd.
Hamlyn House · The Centre · Feltham · Middlesex
© The Hamlyn Publishing Group Ltd 1967
Printed in Italy by Officine Grafiche Arnoldo Mondadori, Verona

Contents

Introduction

Viewed from a twentieth century standpoint, Watteau is one of the most elusive of painters. At first sight there seems to be little connection between his world of music parties, pilgrimages to the Isle of Love, and endless conversations in a garden setting, and life as most people live it today. It is perhaps only fair to say that very few people lived this life in the eighteenth century, or indeed at any time, ever: for all Watteau's clear-eyed observation of gesture and detail his fantasy is stronger than the world around him, which he sees as a point of departure rather than a point of reference. The women he paints have a sparkling miniature solidity, the men an engaging quirkiness, a sharpness of knee, an intense turn of the head which prompt admiration for Watteau's realism; yet these sharp little characters who, even in repose, seem always to be pouting, to be urging, to be inclining their tiny thoughtful heads, exist in a vacuum of apparent purposelessness. Their clothes, of satin slick as the oil into which Watteau translates them, are beautiful, flimsy, and bizarre; the context in which their languid activities take place is grandiose and vague, like a stage set. They look, in fact, like a group of professional actors, either warming up half-heartedly for a performance or enjoying a break in rehearsal, falling into a day-dream while a musician improvises softly on his guitar.

One is encouraged in this speculation by the fact that Watteau's characters vary very little from picture to picture. Over and above their family resemblance, they have spasms of exaggerated courtliness and total indifference enjoyed by people who know each other very well and are still intermittently captivated by the parts they play. Occasionally this company gives us the full performance, becomes galvanised into a quadrille, or takes a rowdy curtain call, or plays out, faultlessly and with nobility, its musical comedy pilgrimage to the Isle of Love. At times like these, Watteau thrills us with his immediacy and we have no trouble in joining him. On other occasions — and they are more frequent — we are puzzled and perhaps held at arm's length by the paradox at the heart of Watteau's art, in which youth, health and beauty are becalmed in apparent inertia, bodies of great physical definition disguised in costumes of fantasy, and intimations of grandeur and melancholy held at bay by the perpetual, though sometimes reluctant, enactment of a comedy.

It is just possible that we are still influenced by the Romantic interpretation of Watteau's painting which gained such currency in the nineteenth century and which still obtains today. For Watteau did not dream up this vanished world: he had seen something very like it on the trestle stages of the various Paris fairs and, more illustriously, on the boards of the Hôtel de Bourgogne, later the Théâtre Italien. The Italian Comedians, the most celebrated of the European theatrical troupes of the later seventeenth century, shared equal honours in Paris with Molière and his company. Their prestige was unlimited until one inauspicious performance in 1697, when too overt references were made to King Louis XIV's morganatic wife, Mme de Maintenon. The company was banished, and for nearly twenty years theatrical enthusiasts in Paris became increasingly critical of the official theatre, the Comédie Française, and increasingly devoted to the memory of the Italians.

Many small French companies copied the original troupe and mounted comedies of their own, written around the traditional characters of the Italian Comedy: Pantalone the merchant, and his friend the Doctor; Isabella and Orazio, the noble, sighing lovers; Arlecchino the acrobatic servant, in his distinctive diamond-patterned costume; Scapino or Mezzetino the musician of the troupe; and Pedrolino, the guileless unfortunate from whom nothing is really hidden, and who has come down to us as Pierrot. These characters move constantly through Watteau's pictures. The noble, rather high-nosed, face of Isabella, constantly crossed in love, is the mask assumed by nearly every one of his dreamingly preoccupied women. Mezzetino is the knobbly, knowing accompanist of a dozen music parties, while Pierrot, in his white jacket and breeches, eventually achieves something not far short of beatification.

After the Italian players, under the direction of Luigi Riccoboni, returned to Paris in 1716, Watteau gave further proof of his partisanship by painting two pairs of pictures contrasting the styles of the Italian and French players, always to the latter's disadvantage. One set compares the evenly lit disposition of the French company with a scene of the Italians playing at night in a mysterious and evocative blaze of candles. The titles given to these pictures are, significantly, *L'Amour au Théâtre Français* and *L'Amour au Théâtre Italien* (plates 22 and 23). Another pair, the largest, most naturalistic and most highly finished pictures painted by Watteau, are a veritable lesson in style. The French scene (plate 45) is a satirical rendering of a tragedy, conveyed, miraculously, down to the dramatically necessary presence of the confidants, and this is contrasted with a curtain-call at the Italian Comedy, which shows the breathless, grinning troupe crushed on to the stage and obviously so well received that even Pierrot permits himself to smile (plate 46).

The Italian Comedy, broad, cruel, gay, and relying on virtuoso individual improvisations on stock situations within a fairly skeletal framework, might well provide the key to to the inspiration of Watteau's art and to its iconography. But there are signs that Watteau, like one of the players, made his own improvisations. That he was enamoured of the world of the theatre is quite clear; even a fairly meretricious comedy like *Les Trois Cousines* by the contemporary dramatist Florent Dancourt, was milked of its moment of poetry which, in time, became the picture known as *L'Embarquement pour l'Ile de Cythère* or *The Embarkation for the Isle of Love*. And this process was repeated, either consciously or uncon-

sciously, on many other occasions. The operation of fantasy transformed the theatre of fact; the personal nostalgia of the artist turned a popular number into an apotheosis. Moreover, like an impresario, Watteau takes liberties with costume and character. The highly traditional clothes of the Comedy players become slightly more languorous and aristocratic as Watteau grafts on to them the ampler skirts, the wider ruffs and the richer satins to be found in the great pictures by Rubens which he was able to study in the Luxembourg Palace. Then, having reclothed his characters, and given them far more distinction than they originally possessed, he isolates them, relegating to the background those for whom he feels no particular interest.

Thus Pantalone and the Doctor, stable props of any Commedia performance, make only a brief appearance on the extreme edge of Watteau's pictures. Isabella is permanently separated from her lover, and even Arlecchino is ultimately overshadowed by the two minor characters for whom Watteau reserves his most intense feelings: Pierrot, often called Gilles in the French companies, and Mezzetino. In an astonishing picture painted at the very end of his life, the Louvre *Gilles* (plate 47), Watteau elevates this dull-witted innocent to quasi-tragic status, to the status of the *Pierrot lunaire* beloved of the nineteenth century. In a no less astonishing picture, the *Mezzetin* (plate 37), the wily companion of Harlequin has become a fastidious commentator, idealistic and at the same time disabused. These characterisations, so intensely thought out that they have become in our minds theatrically more valid than the originals, bring us back to the dualism that has puzzled students of Watteau since his own times: a fantasy of hermetic secrecy with its roots in the most popular entertainment of the day.

There is therefore some justification for the legend of mystery and romance that has grown up around the name of Watteau. This legend, which was promulgated by various nineteenth-century men of letters, has become so tenacious that nowadays we tend to remember first and foremost that Watteau died young, that he was tubercular, and that he was a strange, withdrawn and isolated character who imposed on the extrovert Parisian society, in which he spent the most productive years of his life, a highly idiosyncratic personal vision which is still not fully explained or understood.

In the Romantic period Watteau was co-opted by writers like Théophile Gautier and Gérard de Nerval as an outstanding sufferer from *le mal du siècle*, and it is true that his earliest biographers, most of whom knew him personally, described him as 'indifferent, cold, impatient, timid, sarcastic, rancorous, and always discontented with himself and with others' — qualities which would recommend themselves in the age of the Romantic hero. They might have added that he was conscious of this general malaise, for the self-portrait drawing at Chantilly (see frontispiece) shows a character who views the world with no confidence whatever.

As the nineteenth century wore on, and the sun appeared to set on the world of leisure, privilege and individualism, Watteau was promoted in two contradictory ways. To the eager readers of fashion and domestic magazines he became the advocate and representative of aristocratic taste, and many 'Watteau' touches, usually mass-produced, were introduced in the 1840s into the bourgeois home. At the other end of the scale Edmond and Jules de Goncourt, writing in the teeth of what they considered to be middle-class vulgarity, turned him into an invalid of genius predestined to remind later generations of the golden age of aristocratic fantasy, from which those less happily born are automatically disbarred. In their very brilliant chapter on Watteau in *L'Art du dix-huitième siècle*, the Goncourts sigh ostentatiously for a vanished world of conspicuous waste in which all the work is done somewhere off-stage and the more important moments of life are given over to love and dalliance. Yet in this same

chapter the Goncourts achieve a much more astonishing empathy with the painter than many more rigorous scholars could hope to do. Their study, bristling with exclamation marks, furious with nostalgia, contains a sentence which is as prophetic as it is perceptive. Speaking of *L'Embarquement pour l'Île de Cythère*, they say: 'C'est l'amour, mais c'est l'amour poétique, l'amour qui songe et qui pense, l'amour moderne avec ses aspirations et sa couronne de mélancolie.' ('It is love, but poetic love, love which dreams and reflects, modern love with its aspirations and its crown of melancholy.') This perhaps explains the eternal fascination of Watteau: a modernist in his own times, he has remained essentially modern in his awareness of those doubts which for many obscure the certainties of life.

Yet it must be said that in comparison with the Watteau legend, the facts of Watteau's life are quite brisk. Far from being a social outcast, as the legend would suggest, he was loyally supported by many indulgent friends who bought his pictures the minute he had finished them and who were only too willing to lodge him in their own houses, introduce him to wealthy patrons, and generally smooth his path not only in society but through the thickets of academic advancement. So assiduous were Watteau's friends that he frequently changed his lodgings in order to take a rest from them and seems to have let slip a few unendearing observations in the process. This crankiness, which his devoted friends hastened to ascribe to his illness or possibly to his provincial origins, was Watteau's outstanding characteristic.

Much has been made of the fact that he entered the glossy arena of Paris society in the last years of the reign of Louis XIV as an outsider. He was a native of Valenciennes which, only six years before his birth, in 1684, had been part of the Spanish Netherlands. The town was ceded to France by the Treaty of Nijmegen, but Watteau's contemporaries regarded him as a Flemish artist rather than a French one, a fact con-

2 Rubens *Coronation of Marie de' Medici*
3 Rubens *La Kermesse*

veniently reinforced by his later admiration for Rubens — although it should be pointed out that no self-respecting painter of Watteau's generation, the generation which reacted against the classical style of the second half of the seventeenth century, felt anything less than total veneration for Rubens, who represented the freedom that might be achieved by an emphasis on colour rather than drawing as a means of pictorial description.

Watteau himself was humbly born and his early years are obscure. He was apprenticed to a local painter named Gérin, of whom nothing is known, and then moved on to another master, equally faceless, who was occasionally employed as a scene painter at the Paris Opéra. Perhaps for this reason they both moved to Paris, arriving in 1702, and according to the biographical account written by Jullienne, Watteau worked as assistant to the faceless one, who may have been called Métayer, until the latter became discouraged and 'went home'.

Watteau, stranded in Paris without employment or protection, drifted into the dreariest of jobs: he painted copies of popular favourites such as Gérard Dou's *Old Woman Reading* or Albani's *Seasons* for a quick commercial sale, in which capacity he was fed and lodged like an apprentice in any other trade. At the same time he made contact with the Flemish colony in Paris and also with many dealers in, and collectors of, prints and pictures. Eventually he had the good fortune to meet Claude Gillot, the first of his important contacts in Paris.

Gillot, like Watteau's second master, was connected with the theatre, but in a much more personal way. He had a vast enthusiasm for the Italian Comedy and those of his pictures that have survived are brisk topical scenes from recent or contemporary plays. They are completely without mystery or beauty, but have a graphic journalistic quality that becomes a positive aid to dating. The *Scène des deux Carrosses*

(figure 6), for example, exactly reproduces an incident from a pantomime performed by the Italian players for the first time in December 1695 — this particular scene was added after the first performance — and successfully re-enacted by a native French company on many occasions after that date. There is no doubt that it was through the medium of Gillot that Watteau came to centre his art on the world of the theatre — so successfully that Gillot eventually abandoned the genre and became a full-time engraver and illustrator. The coarse flat style of Gillot's paintings is worlds removed from the eventual refinement and sophistication of Watteau's mature handling, but a study of Gillot's drawings, pointed, quirky, nervous and energetic, reveals a much closer link between the two artists.

The dates of Watteau's apprenticeship with Gillot are not known. The period is generally assumed to have lasted about four years, from about 1703 to 1707, and was brought to a close by Gillot himself, who out of either jealousy or generosity advised Watteau to find another master and tipped him on to Claude III Audran.

Audran holds a distinguished position in the history of the decorative arts. He was a member of a prolific and immensely talented family of painters, decorators and engravers, and was, at the time when Watteau became his assistant, employed at many royal residences, where he introduced a light cursive style of arabesque in sharp contrast to the heavy rectangular and architectonic forms of traditional Louis XIV decoration. His decorative schemes for Marly, for example, are so delicate and calligraphic in character that they give the appearance of being doodled away with a fine crayon (figure 7). It was thus Watteau's good fortune to work with yet another astute modernist, rather than to owe his advancement to one of the more serious and traditional painters still working in the shadow of the Academy.

As Audran's assistant, Watteau was required to paint the

tiny figures planted at the very heart of the complex of arabesques ordered to decorate the walls of both royal and private apartments of which Audran had a virtual monopoly at this time. In at least one of these decorative undertakings, one in which Audran may have allowed him to work on his own, Watteau gives the first signs of his singular originality, for at the royal château of La Muette the tiny figures in one of the rooms are in the Chinese style, and they appear to be among the earliest — if they are not indeed the earliest — examples of this style in France. The figures are not totally convincing, and credit for the scheme, which is now known only from engravings, may be due to Audran, but some of Watteau's basic seriousness emerges from the fact that he went to the trouble of consulting the illustrated books of those Jesuit missionaries who had been to Peking in order to give a certain authenticity to his painted characters.

The years with Audran were important in another way, for Audran was concierge or curator of the Luxembourg Palace which housed the great cycle of pictures painted by Rubens for Marie de Medici between 1621 and 1625. These works were perhaps the weightiest single factor in Watteau's development, because through them he renewed contact with his Flemish origins and became acquainted with the glamour and elegance of one of the most worldly and sophisticated painters in the history of European art. The richly fleshy and colouristic character of Rubens' style plumped out a manner which may have threatened to dwindle into miniature terms. The very setting of the Luxembourg Gardens, less rigid, more poetic than the majority of French gardens of the day, nourished Watteau's imagination, and he made numerous drawings of both the park and the pictures — drawings which, according to his habit, he put into an album and referred to from time to time for the rest of his working life.

The example of Rubens may have encouraged Watteau to complete his artistic education, for in 1709 he presented himself at the Royal Academy of Painting and entered for the Rome prize contest with an Old Testament subject, *David and Nabal*, which, like most of his early work, is now lost. At the same time he sold to a dealer named Sirois a picture showing a *Departure of Troops*, apparently a souvenir of the garrison atmosphere of his home town, Valenciennes. He came only second in the Rome prize contest, but Sirois advanced him a sum of money to paint a pendant to the military scene and he paid a brief and obviously discouraging visit to Valenciennes, possibly to see his family, possibly to work up this genre which he exploited for a short period. By 1710 he was back in Paris, lodging with the obliging Sirois and his family with whom he stayed for two years.

In 1712, in circumstances of mysterious and almost dreamlike ease, he applied for and obtained membership of the Academy. This was a twofold process: associate membership was granted on presentation of one or more pictures, and the successful candidate went on to prepare a specially painted examination piece for full membership. For the first stage of the proceedings Watteau presented the two military pictures painted for Sirois, and the artist De La Fosse sponsored his application. At the same time Watteau undertook to execute within two years a picture which would qualify him for full membership of the Academy. He was allowed to pick his own subject, and he chose, singularly enough, a scene from a recent play (we should describe it as a musical comedy) by Dancourt, of which he had already done an experimental version. This eventually ripened into his most famous work, the picture known by the title of *The Embarkation for the Isle of Love*.

But in fact five years, rather than the statutory two, elapsed before Watteau fulfilled this commission. It seems likely that he delayed because he still hoped to make the Italian journey which had so far eluded him and which was thought indispensable to a painter's education. At the same time he was considerably occupied with other commissions, for he had become immensely popular, and far from being relieved by this state of affairs he became more and more harassed by his lack of privacy. Besieged by collectors and worried by the fading prospect of a journey to Italy, he was therefore more than disposed to accept a commission from the millionaire collector, Pierre Crozat, who wanted a series of paintings of *The Seasons* to decorate a room of his house in the rue de Richelieu. The advantage to Watteau was twofold: by moving in with Crozat he acquired a new home (and Watteau liked to find his homes ready-made for him), and he gained access to Crozat's staggering collection of Old Master drawings which constituted a veritable Italian journey in their own right.

We have no dates for the association with Crozat, apart from the outside limits of 1712 and June 1715, when a Swedish visitor, Carl Gustaf Tessin, noted in his diary that Watteau was living on the Quai de Conti. One of the early biographers notes that this stay was brief. Perhaps, in the shadow of such fulsome patronage, Watteau manifested some of his famous 'discontent'. But he absorbed a general awareness of the works of Veronese, Giacomo Bassano and Campagnola, which gave his style a short-lived Italian finish. He was enabled to make a closer study of Rubens and Van Dyck, which gave a heavier, more sonorous quality to his handling. Last but not least, and in much the same way that the Luxembourg Gardens had once been as important to him as the contents of the Luxembourg Palace, he retained a fruitful memory of the society he had observed in the gardens of Crozat's country house, Montmorency, near Enghien, where the guests strolled or rested in delicious inertia in the dying afternoon.

Documentation seems to increase as Watteau's life draws to a close. On August 28th, 1717, he became a full member of the Academy on the strength of his Cythera picture, but instead of being placed in one of the usual categories — history painter, landscape painter, genre painter, etc. — he was enrolled as *peintre de fêtes galantes*, and thus had the distinction of having a category named after him. This argues that at least some of the great *fêtes galantes* were already painted and had become famous at this date, and that the Academy was ratifying an existing state of affairs rather than inaugurating an era of greater flexibility, as is sometimes claimed. We might therefore be correct in supposing, as indeed common sense suggests, that the *Embarquement* represents the final flowering of this particularly gallant and stately period of Watteau's production, a hypothesis partly borne out by the fact that the second version of this picture, tougher and more deliberate in character, seems to have been painted in a far more objective and business-like mood, as if Watteau had already travelled past the experience and had no particular interest in maintaining it. He still managed to avoid living anywhere on his own account. From Crozat's house he had gone back to Sirois, and then in 1718 and 1719 he shared lodgings with his friend Vleughels, the fat man who points his toe so pompously in the picture called *Les Fêtes Vénitiennes* (plate 35).

Then, in August 1719, he went to England. Little is known of this English visit, which lasted for nearly a year. Tradition has it that he wanted to consult the celebrated Dr Mead about his lung condition, which was now far advanced, but equally tenacious rumours suggest that he had become rather grasping. Perhaps the English were willing to pay more for his pictures than the French? The smoke of London aggravated his malady, but his desperately bad health is nowhere reflected in the work of this time — rather the opposite. In London he painted for Dr Mead the singularly robust picture of the Italian players, to which reference has already been made, while the Wallace Collection

La Toilette (plate 42), also said to have been painted in England, has an earthiness that is surprising to eyes accustomed to the misty poetry of the *fêtes galantes*. It is as if Watteau, faced with certain death, felt a hunger for the realities of this world rather than for those fantasies which had filled his imagination in less precarious days.

On his return to Paris at the end of 1720 he was taken in by Edmé Gersaint, the son-in-law of his old friend Sirois, who was also a picture dealer with a flourishing business called 'A l'Enseigne du Grand Monarque'. With unusual politeness, Watteau asked if he might paint a sign for Gersaint's shop 'to keep his fingers from getting stiff', and in a very short time (though not necessarily the eight days recorded by Gersaint) he finished the miraculous *Enseigne de Gersaint* (plate 44) which was bought within a fortnight by a distinguished collector. Watteau's personal distress was now grave, but he continued to paint. Finally a friend suggested that he might be more comfortable away from Paris and lent him his house at Nogent-sur-Marne. The local priest visited him in an attempt to make his last days tolerable (or intolerable — accounts differ) and in order to please this man, Watteau destroyed a number of pictures and drawings of nudes which he thought might give offence. At the same time he embarked on a painting of *Christ on the Cross*, which is now lost. He intended to go home to Valenciennes, but died before he could make the journey, on July 18th, 1721, at the age of thirty-seven.

Somewhere between the Watteau legend and the facts of Watteau's life lies the truth of his character as an artist, and this is singularly difficult to evaluate. We know little of his work before 1712, he gave his pictures no dates, and the titles, by which they are known were added after his death when his friend Jullienne had his entire production engraved as an act of piety. Moreover, Watteau destroyed a certain amount of what he considered to be uncharacteristic before he died, thus consolidating the myth that he painted only one kind of picture throughout his life. Much of his work is lost: the *David and Nabal* painted for the Rome prize contest, the last *Crucifixion*, the various *morceaux historiés* praised posthumously by Jullienne, and all his early genre scenes. Even the decorative paintings done in connection with Audran, theoretically the most easily traceable of all his early works, are only just beginning to come to light. It is thus too easy on the basis of what remains to classify him, as was done by the Academy in 1717, as a painter of *fêtes galantes*, and to petrify him inside the limits of this not very ambitious genre.

Yet Watteau was no thin-blooded dreamer wedded to the dying fall. His life drawings alone would serve to demonstrate this, while the theatre pictures painted at the end of his life intimate that he was on the brink of a period of far greater realism, and that had he lived he would have altered his scale, broadened his handling, adopted a weightier subject-matter. Some of the pictures, such as the scene of the French actors (plate 45), even imply that somewhere in Watteau's make-up there may have been a full-blooded satirist, not so much fighting to get out as biding his time until he should choose to emerge. And what are we to make of that mysterious year in England, of which so little is known? Were the pictures painted there, for immediate sale, in his recognisably nostalgic style; or were they erotic, scabrous, even pornographic? A curious picture called *La Toilette Intime* in a French private collection permits this last speculation; a detail, otherwise inexplicable, in the bottom left-hand corner of the Dresden *Réunion Champêtre* seems to support it. It is possible that if Watteau had not died so young and that if a second flowering had taken place along the lines suggested by the extant works of 1720–21, the whole course of eighteenth-century French painting would have been changed. Instead of remaining artificially fixed within a Rococo framework it would have been larger, more naturalistic, and perhaps tied to a more ambitious type of subject-matter.

In the absence of evidence, all judgement on Watteau must therefore be provisional. Yet even on the basis of what we know, there is no difficulty in estimating his qualities. One of these is his outstanding modernity. From the date of his arrival in Paris, Watteau, either by accident or design, was able to ignore the grand traditions of seventeenth-century French painting, slightly discredited by the quarrel between the Rubenists and the Poussinists. From this the former emerged triumphant, thus opening the way to painters less hampered by the disciplines of drawing and more open to the fascinations of colour and texture, the more truly descriptive elements in a picture. Trained first by Gillot, an irreverent and independent observer, then by Audran, pioneer of the new style of Rococo decoration, Watteau was almost bound to put to immediate profit his singular opportunity of studying Rubens in the Luxembourg. The prestige of Rubens was then high in France; it was to go higher as painters like Boucher, Greuze and Fragonard followed Watteau's example and demanded permission to study the Luxembourg series. By the same token the timid *chinoiseries* which Watteau essayed at La Muette were to become a French speciality later in the century in the hands of painters like Boucher, Huet, and Pillement, while his surprising decision to use a source book for his representations of Chinese modes and manners was implemented by all who subsequently tried their hand at the Turkish, Russian and eventually Etruscan and Egyptian styles.

These evidences of originality could be explained by ignorance, innocence or pure chance. But later in his life, while under the spell of the desired Italian journey, Watteau does not go back on them. After the new period of apprenticeship in Crozat's collection, in which he had an opportunity virtually to reshape his style, he painted a certain number of mythologies. One of these is the *Jupiter and Antiope* (plate 13) in the Musée du Louvre, which has a more mellifluous, more sophisticated appearance, but he retained the fine, almost miniature scale bred into him by his association with Gillot and Audran. His development was to be in the direction of greater realism, not, as he intended, of greater style. And a mature work, such as *Les Fêtes Vénitiennes* (plate 35), amply demonstrates his lack of respect for some of the clichés of seventeenth-century academic painting, as well as the survival of his allegiance to the iconoclastic spirit of Gillot. To take one small example, the sculpted figure of a naiad is almost mockingly lightweight in character and is sketched in in those small curling rhythms that reflect the current decorative vogue of the Rococo. This point alone would indicate Watteau's attitude to the Poussinists, for the importance of sculpture, whether three-dimensional or painted, was a plank of the academic platform. The curvilinear outline of the naiad is paralleled in the arc of the fountain and in the double-C curve of the figures. The characters themselves are seized in moments of intimate, almost unreflecting, movement which bears witness to Watteau's affection for the *gravures de modes* (fashion plate engravings) of earlier and more obscure seventeenth-century artists like Picart, Simpol, and Duflos. Indeed, the very isolation of Watteau's characters, into which nineteenth-century writers read such a wealth of psychological significance, may be due to the fact that in his apprenticeship days Watteau had a greater opportunity to study humble examples such as these than to build a style round fully integrated compositions, and that this hazard, like all the others of his formative years, became elevated into personal advantage. The subject of the picture is based, loosely, on the minuet intermezzo in the opera-ballet *Les Fêtes Vénitiennes*, which was performed once a year, every year, from 1710 to about 1740, at the Paris Opéra. The 'action', if it can be

4 Jacques Callot *Courtiers*

so described, is fragmented, self-absorbed and apparently pointless, for Watteau has slightly dislocated whatever unity the scene may have possessed and thus compounded another crime against the Academy, unity of action being another of the desiderata laid down by this body in its recommendations for a well composed picture. Perhaps the bagpipe player is in love with the girl who turns her back on him and dances opposite Watteau's friend Vleughels, who is dressed as some kind of Grand Turk, but the gestures and expressions have a mocking quality which suggests that we should not take this too seriously. As the Grand Turk can be identified as Vleughels, a perceptive scholar has suggested that the bagpipe player may in fact be Watteau himself. Underneath his obviously borrowed (or hired) costume, he appears to be rougher and lumpier in texture than his fellows, and is wearing an expression of haggard benignity which betokens both physical exhaustion and social strain. The implications are obvious and acceptable. The man wearing a cloak and tricorne hat in the background is caught in a deeply theatrical attitude; although nobody is looking at him he is about to make a resounding exit. Odd items of Commedia dell'Arte costume can be detected here and there in the audience — a hat, a ruff, a green satin doublet — but the setting has been turned into something totally straight-

16

forward: a clearing in one of the *allées* of any of the great woods around Paris. One need go no farther than Sceaux, Saint-Cloud or Versailles to find an identical spot today. And the final impression of the picture is not of a flight of fancy but of absolutely matter-of-fact and slightly off-beat realism. The visual oddities are presented for our scrutiny, not for our acceptance. We are not required to understand them; we are simply enabled to appreciate that satin skirt, that fringe of water, that sunlight in the distance, and to become absorbed by them.

The same becalmed nonchalance, baffling to anyone seeking for subject or time sequence, is apparent in the Wallace Collection *Music Party* (plate 31), the Potsdam *Concert* (plate 33), the Louvre *Assemblée dans un Parc* (plate 24) and many others. These pictures represent a high plateau of spiritual ease: it is no accident that Baudelaire spoke of the 'illustrious hearts' of Watteau's characters. One step behind them in the story of Watteau's development are the tiny vigorous studies in which the artist is still greedy for physiognomical accuracy and detail, studies like the portrait of *Sirois and his Family* (plate 15), in which every knuckle and nostril is palpable. One step forward and Watteau embarks on the full and elaborate composition, as in the two Cythera pictures (plates 26 and 29), the *Italian Players* (plate 46), or *L'Enseigne de Gersaint* (plate 44). These great set-pieces, which are not exactly typical of the fragmented world of Watteau, nevertheless sum up and present in concentrated form the various components of his style and of his singularity. The Louvre *Cythère*, in particular, has called forth more coloratura prose than any other picture of similar importance in the entire spectrum of French painting, and it has long been a vehicle for fantasies less distinguished and more explicit than Watteau's own. Its obvious glamour, rendered down from the fleshy opulence of Rubens, in pictures such as the *Jardin d'Amours* at Dresden, and its obvious

beauty, which is an affair of highly sophisticated mannered figures being overwhelmed and made poignant by the greenish light of a dying day, now lie locked in yellow varnish yet still act as a magnet to Romantics of all ages.

More tendentious spirits may be satisfied by the fact that the picture is precisely datable, that it reflects the maximum number of influences, and that it appears to be the most purely theatrical of all Watteau's *fêtes galantes*. In fact, and this is fairly unusual in Watteau's work, it is a picture whose genealogy can be explained. In 1700 Paris saw for the first time a comedy by Dancourt called *Les Trois Cousines*, which closed with a rather elaborate divertissement — a girl dressed as a pilgrim stepped out of a chorus of other girls similarly attired and invited the audience to join them on a journey to the Isle of Love:

Venez dans l'Île de Cythère	Join us on our pilgrimage to
En pèlerinage avec nous…	the Isle of Cythera,
L'on y fait sa grande affaire	where one's destiny is sealed
Des amusements les plus doux…	by the sweetest of pleasure…
Pour s'engager dans ce voyage	No formalities are needed
Il ne faut pas tant de façons;	for this journey:
Je ne veux pour tout équipage	all I take are my love
Que mon amour et mon bourdon.	and my pilgrim's staff.

The play was revived in 1709 and at about this time or shortly after, Watteau painted the scene as it must have appeared during the singing of this very important song. The picture (plate 9), shows the girls with their pilgrim staves and shells lining up to embark for the Island of Love. No attempt is made to alter the pantomime effect of the original and our viewpoint is that of an audience in the stalls given an uninterrupted view of the stage.

Several mysterious years elapsed between the painting of this picture and the Louvre *Embarquement pour l'Île de Cythère* (plate 27), and so enormous was the painter's gain in sophistication during these years that, far from having the naive simplicity of the early picture, the Louvre work is still the subject of learned commentary. Firstly, the time sequence: are the pilgrims about to embark for the Island, or are they about to leave Cythera and return to their homes? Support has been given to the first idea by the fact that the disposition of the action exactly conforms to that of the earlier picture; support to the second by the fading evening light and the statue of Venus, emblem of love, bedecked with votive flowers. A second point is the great variety of influences reflected in the painting, which show how Watteau benefited from his study of Crozat's collection: the rounded Rubensian forms; the composition itself, which may have been suggested by a drawing by the seventeenth-century Flemish artist Jordaens, now in the British Museum; the vaguely cosmic landscape, from Leonardo or Campagnola; and the high, tipped viewpoint, common in the works of sixteenth-century Flemish landscapists, Brueghel, Momper, and Savery.

Yet, having paid full attention to these matters, one has still not touched the true achievement of Watteau in this picture which is, on the formal level, the animation of a perfect Rococo movement, and on the spiritual level the attempt to create a mythology for modern times. That statue of Venus, the only element of mystery in the entire composition, is not patron of the festival. Having paid their token offerings, the pilgrims give her no further attention. The rigidity of her figure underlines the more exaggerated of their gestures — that of the man at the stern of the boat, for example — and her blind head, with its enigmatic expression, might almost be the ancestress of the impassive goddesses of Vigny and Baudelaire. As to that tender rocking rhythm, which, reading the picture from left to right, curves towards one, away from one, towards one and aways again,

and which from right to left meanders into the S and C curves of the Rococo arabesque, here is the fullest realisation in human terms of a formula normally reserved for the accessories of life but given new significance in this exceptional transposition.

When Jullienne, Watteau's friend, asked for a copy of the picture, Watteau painted him something far more winning, tougher, more calculated. Jullienne's version, now in Berlin (plate 29), charms by its brilliant enamelled surface, its deeper, more exciting rhythms. But one notices with some dismay that an element of vulgarity has crept in. The twisting, bending Venus and the swarms of putti are outrunners of that Olympian demi-monde that was to lower the tone of much of later eighteenth-century French painting. The transition to the less abstruse fantasies of Boucher and Fragonard and their followers is here made visible.

Having created the rare mood of the Louvre version, Watteau sensibly did not seek to prolong it. If this were the last picture he had painted we should be fully justified in accepting his legend and allowing the Goncourts to be his final apologists. But in his last years Watteau takes on another character. He paints pictures which, when they are not actually larger in scale, are composed of larger forms, and are much broader, more direct, in feeling. That curious picture of the French actors (plate 45), a pendant to the *Italian players* painted in England for Dr Mead, is a case in point. It appears to be a satire on the reigning stage personalities of the days, for the figure in black on the right seems to be something out of Molière, while the four protagonists are clearly enacting a scene from Racine. All the stuffy panoply of the Comédie Française is here: the palace setting (obligatory), the padded hips, the powdered hair, the over-emphatic utterance which appeared so rigid and old-fashioned when compared with the irreverent naturalism of the Italians. Perhaps the image of the heroine, Mlle Duclos,

5 Jacques Callot *Soldiers*

who is well launched on her aria of self-justification, owes something to Largillière's portrait of the great tragedienne as Ariadne. In any event, Watteau sees her as an impressive but not notably alluring figure; his modernity gives no quarter to this type of tradition.

In the war of styles waged between the French and Italian players, it is clear on whose side Watteau finds himself. And if it were not apparent from this picture alone, additional evidence could be found in the *Gilles* (plate 47), one of the last pictures he ever painted and certainly one of the most extraordinary.

The history of the *Gilles* is as inscrutable as the expression on the clown's face. The picture is undated, no drawings exist, and it was never engraved. Compared with Watteau's habitual scale it is gigantic, and the handling is broad and matt. All these factors reinforce something suggested by the subject-matter — namely, that it was probably a theatre billboard, painted for one of those small French companies which set up in emulation of the Italians. Although they followed the main outline of the Commedia dell'Arte repertory, the French players created variations of their own, including a character named Gilles, a modification of the original

6 Claude Gillot *Scènes des deux Carrosses*

Pierrot, whose existence is first noted in 1695. This character, whose final incarnation was as Pagliacci, was the natural unfortunate of the troupe, the butt of its most brutal comic sallies, but protected by an armour of innocence which was eventually seen to triumph. To the keen appetites of the eighteenth-century audience the whole point of Gilles was his thick-headedness, his ability to resist instruction. In a popular performance attempt would be made to knock some sense into him; he would be given a dancing master, a fencing master, a drawing master — all to no avail. At this point of the action a donkey would be led across the stage to underline his ineffable stupidity. This is the moment painted by Watteau. But as well as recording a moment of theatrical history, Watteau has again given the situation a colouring of his own. For his Gilles belongs in a more contemplative setting than that of knockabout farce. The impassivity of the face suggests that the ability to survive continuous if light-hearted cruelty is not only potentially tragic but at all times heroic. This is a concept worthy of Watteau, who has given rise to comments, from Voltaire among others, that he never painted anything serious. The *Gilles* is not only one of the most serious pictures to be painted in the eighteenth century, it is perhaps the most truly personal of all Watteau's works.

The gift of transforming a *fait divers* into a unique personal creation is not a common one. *Madame Bovary* was originally a paragraph in a provincial newspaper; *L'Enseigne de Gersaint* once hung outside the Paris picture dealer's shop called 'A l'Enseigne du Grand Monarque'. And, slyly, Watteau has even put the *grand monarque* — Louis XIV — in his sign, but, unimpressed as always by this kind of reference, he is having his effigy packed out of sight in a delivery crate. The analogy with Flaubert's newspaper cutting is relevant here, for the particular format of Watteau's picture — one wall removed from a room which is seen in steep perspective —

was used in at least one other known contemporary shop sign. But its original purpose pales into insignificance when one sees it today, so much so that we scrutinise it as if it held the key to a vanished civilisation. Certain human factors are recognisable: the archetypal figure of the connoisseur, kneeling with his nose to the canvas, has survived unmodified through the centuries. It is a paradox that this, the most aristocratic of Watteau's pictures, should have been the most humble in intention, that this *musée imaginaire* was perhaps no more than a flattering reference to Gersaint's stock, embellished with a few aesthetic memories from Watteau's own private store. There is very little fantasy here and more than an element of satire, but above all a gravity that is unusual. Here again, those critics of Watteau's 'frivolity' prove how singularly they were led astray by some of his lighter pieces.

Watteau estranges those who look at his pictures as he once estranged his friends. Even when he was dead he produced strong feelings of exasperation in persons of a literal turn of mind and managed to remain as much of a mystery as he had been in life. The history of his reputation is still a little baffling for it has been constantly animated by involuntary currents of like and dislike. His pupils Lancret and Pater were not notably talented and may have contributed to the decline in Watteau's popularity in the eighteenth century. Even Diderot, whose love of painting was so carnivorous that it might be more accurately described as lust, could not take to him at all and dismissed him out of hand with the words, 'I would give ten Watteaus for a Teniers'. This might be understood as the fate of an intensely topical painter momentarily displaced by the vogue for other intensely topical or fashionable painters. But this would imply that Watteau is rootless — yet we are convinced that he is also an Old Master. What is the answer? It may possibly lie in a sentence written by Watteau's friend, the soldier

7 Claude III Audran *Singerie*

Antoine de la Roque, who stated in 1721 that Watteau's pictures contained 'an agreeable mixture of the serious, the grotesque, and the caprices of both *traditional and contemporary French taste*'.

In other words Watteau not only invents, he revives. But what he revives is, on different occasions, the pure, sweet and melancholy style of Primaticcio and the School of Fontainebleau, and the sharp, incisive grotesques drawn and engraved by Jacques Callot, although it is only fair to say that Gillot had done this before him. He ignores as if it had never existed the greatest age of French civilisation, the latter half of the seventeenth century, which laid down the rules and patterns for all the arts, notably the arts of painting and drama. He bundles Louis XIV out of sight, as do the packers in Gersaint's shop; he is less than courteous to the noble actors of the Comédie Française. This provincial invalid manifests a calm disregard for tradition which is in itself fairly awe-inspiring. He remains unmoved by his audacities and gives no explanation for not emulating his elders, the honoured French practitioners of his chosen craft. It is this quality of impassivity, of incommunicability, that exasperated Diderot as it has many lesser men. One must add to this the hazards that attend the reputation of an iconoclast who is accustomed to, and who accustoms his public to thinking in negative terms — for example, he is against this, he does not admire that, he remains uninfluenced by the other, and so on. It was only when the eighteenth century became a moment in history, when it achieved equal status, so to speak, with the seventeenth, that the Romantics discovered in this very wryness the gravity of a vanished era. The great renaissance of Watteau's popularity became linked with the fervent regrets of his nineteenth-century apologists. It is to be hoped that in due course the critical spirit of the twentieth century will do him similar justice.

Biographical outline

1684 Born in Valenciennes, technically a Flemish city until 1678, when it was ceded to France under the terms of the Treaty of Nijmegen.

c. 1700 Apprenticed first to a local painter named Gérin, and then to the equally obscure Métayer.

1702 Watteau's second master brings him to Paris and then abandons him. Watteau paints trade copies of popular favourites.

c. 1703 Meets Claude Gillot, whose pupil and assistant he becomes.

1707-8 On the advice of Gillot, Watteau seeks another master, and is employed as assistant by Claude III Audran, decorative designer and curator of Luxembourg Palace.

1708-9 Watteau assists Audran and even produces original designs for decoration of rooms in royal houses of Marly and La Muette, and private houses such as the Hôtel de Nointel in the rue de Lille, Paris. Studies paintings by Rubens in Luxembourg.

1709 Enters for the Academy's Rome prize with a picture of *David and Nabal* (now lost) and comes 1709.

1709 Short visit to Valenciennes: military subjects.

1710 Paris, lodging with Sirois, a dealer who owns a *Departure of Troops* painted by Watteau in second.

1712 Becomes associate member (*agréé*) of the Academy. Popular with private patrons; numerous commissions.

1712-15 Association with Pierre Crozat, vastly wealthy patron and collector. Watteau paints *The Seasons* for the dining room of his house in the rue de Richelieu; stays intermittently at rue de Richelieu and visits Crozat's country house, Montmorency, near Enghien; and above all avails himself of Crozat's fabulous collection, making a particular study of Rubens, Van Dyck, Titian, Giacomo Bassano, Campagnola, and Parmigianino.

1715 June Watteau living on Quai de Conti, Paris.

1717 August 28th Becomes full member (*reçu*) of the Academy with *L'Embarquement pour l'Ile de Cythère*. Enrolled as *peintre de fêtes galantes*. Lodging with Sirois.

1718 Lodging with Vleughels, rue du Cardinal Lemoine.

1720-21 (Caylus says Watteau left Paris at end of 1719.) He went to London, ostensibly to consult Dr Mead about his chest. Gersaint says Watteau lost his money (presumably in the South Sea Bubble affair); so he may have stayed in London to recoup his loss. Painted *Italian Comedians* for Dr Mead (in payment for his services?).

1721 Paris, lodging with Gersaint, son-in-law of Sirois. Watteau paints his shop sign (*l'Enseigne de Gersaint*). Gravely ill, he moves to Nogent, intending to rest before going home to Valenciennes. Destroys many studies of nudes; starts on a picture of *Christ on the Cross*.
On or about July 18th Watteau dies at the age of thirty-seven.

Comments on Watteau

The graceful and elegant painter whose death we are announcing was highly distinguished in his profession, and his memory will always be dear to real lovers of painting. There is no better proof of this than the excessive price that his easel pictures fetch today. He only ever painted pictures of small figures, in the Flemish style, but of which the colour was very close to that of Rubens. He had made a great study of this particular school. He left his drawings and sketches to his friend, the abbé Harancher, canon of Saint-Germain l'Auxerrois, a lover of good pictures, who possesses examples by excellent artists . . .

The genius of this skilful artist inclined him to compose small *sujets galants*: country weddings, dances, masquerades, water parties, etc. The variety of the draperies, hair ornaments and costumes are particularly pleasing in his compositions. These show an agreeable mixture of the serious, the grotesque, and the fantasies of both traditional and contemporary French taste.

Antoine de la Roque,
in the *Mercure de France*, August, 1721

Watteau was of middling height and poor health; he had a quick and penetrating mind and noble feelings; he spoke little but well and wrote in the same manner. He reflected a great deal. A great admirer of nature and of all the masters whom he copied, an excess of work had made him slightly melancholy. His manner was cold and awkward, which made him difficult as far as his friends were concerned, and indeed as far as he himself was concerned, but his only faults were indifference and love of change. It could be said that no painter ever had a greater reputation either during his lifetime or after his death. His pictures, which fetched very high prices, are still eagerly sought after. They are to be found in Spain, in England, in Germany, in Italy, in Prussia, in many parts of France, and above all in Paris.

For this reason alone, it would seem obvious that there are no more agreeable pictures for private apartments than his; they combine correct drawing, true colour, and an inimitable finesse of touch. He had an excellent understanding of landscape. He excelled not only in courtly and open air compositions but in military scenes, route marches and bivouacs, done in a simple, natural style which makes this type of picture highly prized; he even left a few subject pictures (*morceaux historiés*) in such excellent taste that one realises that he could have done just as well in this genre if he had concentrated on it.

Although Watteau's life was very short, the great number of his works might make one think that it had been long, whereas in fact he was simply very hard working. In fact, even his hours of recreation or walking were occupied with studies after nature, which he sketched whenever he came across a particularly striking aspect.

Jean de Jullienne,
Abrégé de la Vie d'Antoine Watteau, 1726 or 1736

. . . up to the time of his journey to England, the instability of his character made him change his home several times, never wanting to stay for long in places which he himself had chosen and looked forward to eagerly. He was very busy during his stay in England: his pictures were highly popular and well paid; it was there that he began to be interested in money, which he had never been in the past, ignoring it to the point of indifference and always thinking that his works fetched more than they deserved . . . his disinterest was so great that on more than one occasion he rebuked me sharply for having wanted to give him a decent price for certain things — a price which, out of sheer generosity, he refused.

. . . On his return to Paris in 1721, when my business was still in its early stages, he came and asked me if I would receive him and allow him, in order to keep his fingers supple — those were his very words — if I would allow him, as I was saying, to paint a sign to be exhibited outside the shop. I was not in favour of the idea because I would have preferred him to work on something more substantial; but seeing that it would give him pleasure, I consented. The success of this picture is well known; it was all done from the life; the attitudes were so varied and so graceful, the composition so natural, and the groups so well thought out that it attracted the attention of passers-by: even highly skilled painters came several times to admire it. It was done in eight days, and even then he only worked in the mornings; his delicate health, or, to be more accurate, his weakness, prevented him from working on it any longer. This was the only work in which he ever took the slightest pride; he told me this quite frankly . . .

After about six months his state of mind, which was the result of a delicate and overburdened temperament, made him think that he would be imposing on me if he stayed any longer. This became obvious and he asked me to find him a suitable lodging. It would have been pointless to refuse: he was strong-willed and brooked no opposition. I did what he asked, but he did not enjoy his new home for very long; his complaint became more grave, his restlessness and impatience increased. He thought he might be better in the country, and indeed insisted on this, and only quietened down when he learnt that M. le Febvre, then *intendant des Menus*, had, on the suggestion of his friend, the late abbé Haranger, canon of S. Germain l'Auxerrois, offered him a retreat in his house at Nogent, near Vincennes. I took him there and went to see him, and comfort him, every two or three days.

The desire for change tormented him once more. He thought he could overcome his illness by deciding to go home; he told me this and in order to expedite the matter asked me to make an inventory of the few things he had

and to sell them, realising 3,000 livres which he entrusted to me. This represented the fruit of his labours, together with 6,000 livres which M. de Jullienne had saved for him from the crash about the time when he left for England, and which were returned to his family after his death, together with the 3,000 livres in my charge.

From day to day he hoped to gather sufficient strength to make the journey on which I was to accompany him; but his weakness increased and, giving way suddenly, he died in my arms at the said Nogent a little after July 18th, 1721, aged 37 years . . .

Watteau was of middling height and poor health; he had an anxious, restless character; dominated by his desires; a libertine in spirit but staid in his way of life, impatient, timid, with a cold awkward manner, discreet and reserved with strangers, a good but difficult friend, misanthropic, even sarcastic and biting, always discontented with himself and with others, and rarely forgiving. He spoke little but well; he loved reading, which was his only recreation, and although uneducated he could pass a fair judgement on a work. This, as far as I have been able to study, is his portrait from life; no doubt his perpetual hard work, the fragility of his temperament and the acute miseries with which his life had been burdened made him difficult and exaggerated the social defects which overshadowed him.

As far as his works were concerned, one would have wished that his early studies had been in the historical style, and that he had lived longer; it is reasonable to suppose that he would have become one of France's greatest painters; his pictures reflect some of the impatience and inconstancy of his character. An object in his field of vision for any length of time irritated him; he had a need to switch from subject to subject; he often began an arrangement already half bored with its perfection. To expedite a composition which he had started and was obliged to finish, he loaded his brush with oil in order to spread the colour more easily; for this reason, it must be admitted, his pictures are rapidly deteriorating, have completely changed colour, or become hopelessly tawny; but those which are free of this fault are admirable and will always hold their own in the finest collections.

Edmé Gersaint,
Catalogue de la collection du feu M. Quentin de Lorangere, 1744

... his character was such that he was nearly always displeased with what he was doing. One of the principal reasons for this was that he had very lofty ideas about painting. I am in a position to state that he saw art as something infinitely superior to what he himself was doing. This made him far from indulgent towards his own works. The money they brought him did not impress him either and was in any case less than he could have got for them. For he had no love of money and was not attached to it. He was therefore not even supported by financial ambition, such a powerful incentive for so many others ...

Enjoying an agreeable reputation, he had no enemy other than himself and a certain instability which dominated him. He was no sooner established in a dwelling than he took against it. He changed and changed about and always on pretexts which, because of his qualms about being reduced to them, he tried to make unusual. He was happiest in certain rooms which I had in various parts of Paris, and which were used for posing the model, painting and drawing. In such places, given over completely to art and free of all importunities, we experienced, he and I, together with a mutual friend, the pure pleasures of youth and the stimulus of imagination, the two faculties joined in the charms of painting. I can say that on these occasions, Watteau, so sombre and sardonic, so timid and caustic in other circumstances,

was exactly like the Watteau of his paintings, or rather the painter his pictures suggest: charming, tender, and perhaps a little romantic.

It was during these sessions that I learnt to my great profit how deeply Watteau thought about painting and how inferior his practice was to his principles. Having no knowledge of anatomy and having hardly ever drawn the nude, he could neither understand it nor express it, to such an extent that an academic arrangement taxed him and for that reason displeased him. Women's bodies, being less clearly articulated, were easier for him. All this comes back to my earlier remark, that his habitual dissatisfaction with his own work was inevitable in a man whose ideas were better than his actual performance ...

Basically, it must be admitted, Watteau was infinitely mannered. Although endowed with certain graces, and seductive in his favourite subjects, his hands, heads, and even his landscapes reflect this failing. Taste and effect are his greatest advantages, and it is true that they produce agreeable illusions, particularly as his colour is good and extremely well suited to the depiction of his draperies, which are interestingly drawn ... As far as expression is concerned I can say little, for he has never risked showing a single passion ... in the normal way he drew without purpose. For he never made a sketch or a study for any of his works, however slight or non-committal. His habit was to put his drawings in a bound volume so that he always had a considerable number to hand. He had a set of fancy costumes, some of them theatrical, with which he clothed his characters of both sexes as and when the situation demanded — characters whom he portrayed in the attitudes in which he found them, the simpler the better. When he wanted to compose a picture he had recourse to his album. He chose from it the figures which best suited his immediate purpose. He arranged them in groups which were usually dictated by a landscape background. He rarely proceeded in any other way.

This method of composition, which is certainly not to be recommended, is the real cause of the uniformity with which Watteau's paintings can be charged. In addition to this, he often repeated the same figure several times, either because it particularly pleased him or because it was the first to come to hand ... To put it briefly, with the exception of certain pictures, such as *The Village Bride* or *Wedding*, the *Ball*, the sign done for Monsieur Gersaint, and the *Embarkation for the Isle of Love* which he painted for his academy reception piece and which he repeated, his compositions have no focus, they do not express any passion, and therefore lack one of the most exciting elements in painting, namely, action.

Comte de Caylus, in a lecture read
to the Royal Academy of Painting,
Paris, February 3rd, 1748

An Englishman whom I met the other day at a picture dealer's made a remark which the French will find deeply embarrassing. After having examined a large number of pictures representing scenes from the Italian Comedy, dances, and *guinguettes*, he asked, 'What do you think of these decorative pieces?'

'I am amazed at their popularity', I replied. 'It makes me wonder whether painting is not really in decline in this country'.

'Your fears are well founded', he said. 'Many people claim that in twenty years time the French will be willing to exchange two Raphaels for a fan by Vateau'.

Jean-Baptiste de Boyer, Marquis d'Argens,
Lettres Juives. Nouvelle edition augmentée.
Vol. 6. The Hague, 1742

I prefer country manners to coquetry and I would give ten Watteaus for a Teniers.

Diderot, *Pensées détachées sur la Peinture, la Sculpture, l'Architecture et la Poésie, pour servir de suite aux Salons*. Published 1798. (*Oeuvres complètes*, ed. Assézat. Paris, Garnier, 1876)

'Watteau, cousin, one of the greatest French painters of the eighteenth century! Here, do you not see the signature?' he said, showing her one of the pastorals in which ladies disguised as peasants and gentlemen disguised as shepherds joined in a dance.

'What movement! What verve! What colours! And done with a flourish, like an exercise by a master calligrapher; one has no feeling of effort ...'

'You!' cried the president, 'one of Servin's most brilliant pupils and you don't know Watteau!'

'I know David, Gérard, Gros and Girodet, and Guérin, and M. de Forbin, and M. Turpin de Crissé ...'

'You ought ...'

'What ought I, Monsieur?' asked the president's wife, giving him a look worthy of the Queen of Sheba.

'You ought to know Watteau, my dear, he is extremely fashionable', replied the president, with a humility which denoted all the obligations he had towards his wife.

Balzac, *Le Cousin Pons*, 1846–47

With Watteau, the trees are done according to a formula: they are always the same trees and they remind one of a theatre décor rather than trees in a forest. A picture by Watteau put beside an Ostade or a Ruysdael loses a great deal. The artificiality becomes glaring. You tire very quickly of the convention, whereas you can't tear yourself away from the Flemish examples.

Journal of Eugène Delacroix, July 29th, 1854

'Do you realise, Monsieur, that Watteau is a very great painter? Do you know his work? It is immense . . . I have it all at home, Monsieur, and I consult it . . . Watteau! Watteau! . . .'

Ingres, in 1834 (quoted by Amaury-Duval in
l'Atelier d'Ingres, Paris, 1924)

Watteau. Despised in David's time and now back in favour. Admirable technique. His fantasy does not stand up to the works of the Flemish school. In comparison with Ostade, Van de Velde, etc., he is simply theatrical.

Delacroix in his *Journal* on January 11th, 1857

The great poet of the eighteenth century is Watteau. A creation, an entire creation of poetry and dream, issuing from his mind, filled his works with the elegance of a supernatural life. From the fantasies of his brain, from the caprices of his art, from his entirely original genius, a thousand spells took wing. The painter has drawn an ideal world from the enchanted visions of his imagination and has built, beyond the limits of his own time, a Shakespearian kingdom, one of those amorous, luminous countries, a paradise of gallantry such as Polyphilus and his like built on the clouds of a dream for the delicate joy of all poetic spirits.

Watteau renewed the quality of grace. But Watteau's grace is no longer the grace of antiquity: an austere and solid charm, the marble perfection of Galatea, the entirely plastic, entirely material appeal of the various representations of Venus. Watteau's grace is grace pure and simple. It is that subtle quality which clothes a woman in an attraction, a coquetry, a beauty that is beyond mere physical beauty. It is that indefinable thing that seems to be the smile of a contour, the soul of a form, the spiritual physiognomy of matter.

All the fascination of woman in repose: the languor, the idleness, the abandon, the leaning against another, the stretchings, the relaxations, the harmony of attitudes, the delightful sight of a profile bent over a *gamme d'amour*, the elusive contours of a breast, the meanderings, the undulations, the pliancies of a female body, and the play of slender fingers on the handle of a fan, and the indiscretion of a high heel peeping below a skirt, and the happy accidents of deportment, and the coquetry of gestures, and the shrugging of shoulders, and all that the women of the last century learnt from their mirrors . . . all this, with its freshness and its own special character, lives on in Watteau, immortalised and fixed for ever in a form more vital than the breast of that wife of Diomedes moulded from the ashes of Pompeii. And this grace was not merely animated by Watteau, freed from immobility, but set in motion, pulsating to a rhythm, its graceful progress almost a dance led on by some unheard harmony.

But why draw imagery from the world's spectacle when one can invent a world and its poetry? The unique and ravishing poetry of leisure, of the conversations and songs of youth, of pastoral recreation and languorous pastime, a poetry of peace and tranquillity where even the movements of a swing die away, its rope dragging on the sand . . . This is Theleme or Tempe, enchanted islands separated from the land by a ribbon of crystal, peaceful and uncultivated islands of shade and repose, of aimless walks, of hours spent leaning on one's elbow contemplating the repose of clouds and waves. Time is eclipsed on the horizon, beneath a rustic roof. In some fortuitous and enchanted spot on the earth's surface there is eternal indolence under the trees. Sight and thought languish in a vague lost distance like those deep impalpable backgrounds that are the frontiers of Titian's pictorial world. Lethe spreads silence through this land of forgetfulness whose inhabitants are all eyes and mouth: such ardour, such smiles! Thoughts and airs and words like the words of Shakespeare's comedies of love tremble on their parted lips; one sees them seated in the shade, souls dressed in satin, enchantresses clothed and christened by poets: Linda and Gulboé, Hero and Rosalind, Viola and Olivia, and all the heroines of *As You Like It*. Flower sellers pass among them providing decoration for bodices and topknots of hair. The only sound is that of dark-eyed children playing, pattering like birds at the feet of loving couples: tiny genius spirits left by the poet on the threshold of this dream or spell. Nothing to do but to listen to one's heart, to let one's spirit speak, to wait for refreshments to be brought, to let the sun go down and the world go by and little girls tease dogs who never bark.

This is Olympus and the new mythology: the Olympus of all the demi-gods forgotten by antiquity. It is the deification of the eighteenth-century ideal, the spirit of the world and of the age of Watteau brought to the Pantheon of human passions and fashions. It is the new emotional temper of an ageing humanity, Languor, Gallantry and Revery given flesh by Watteau in full-dressed allegories. The women, one might say the goddesses, of his paintings are the moral muses of our time.

Love is the light of this world. Love permeates and fills it, is its youth and its serenity. Cross its rivers and its mountains, its paths and its gardens, its lakes and its fountains, and Watteau's paradise opens out before your eyes: Cythera. Beneath a summer sky Cleopatra's barge is moored at the water's edge. There are no waves; the woods are silent. From the grass to the sky, beating the windless air with their butterfly wings, a swarm of Cupids flies and plays and dances, joining the careless couples with garlands of roses, threading the roundels of kisses that mount from earth to heaven. Here is the temple, here is the journey's end of this world: *l'Amour paisible*, Love disarmed, seated in the shade . . . a smiling Arcady, a Decameron of the feelings, a sentimental meditation, a dreamily distracted courtship; words that soothe the spirit, a Platonic gallantry, a leisure given over to things

of the heart, a youthful indolence; a court of amorous pre-occupations, the tender teasing courtesy of newly-weds, leaning towards each other over their linked arms; eyes without hunger, embraces without impatience, desire without lust, pleasure without desire; a boldness of gesture orchestrated like a ballet for the occasion, gestures parried calmly and without haste; the whole chronicle of body and mind appeased, becalmed, resurrected, beatified; an indolence of passion at which the stone satyrs in the green walks laugh their goat's laugh . . .

Those gods have gone, and Rubens, who lives again in this palette of carmine and golden flesh tints, wanders disconcerted through these celebrations, where the tumult of the senses is stilled, animated fantasies which seem to wait for the wave of a wand to lose their corporeal presences and disappear like a midsummer night's dream. It is Cythera, but it is Watteau's own Cythera. It is love; but it is poetic love, a love which dreams and reflects, modern love with its aspirations and its crown of melancholy. Yes, at the heart of Watteau's work, a slow vague harmony informs the laughing words; a musical and imperceptibly contagious sadness steals through his *fêtes galantes*. Like the seduction of Venice, a veiled and yearning poetry speaks in a low voice to the charmed spirit. The man emerges from his works, and you come to see his works as the game and distraction of a suffering mind, like the toys of a sick child, now dead.

As to the man, his portrait tells you all. Here he is as a youth, drawn from the life: an uneasy face, thin and nervous; arched, restless brows; large, dark, mobile eyes; a long thin nose; a sad mouth, sharply drawn; a deep line running from the nostrils to the corners of the mouth. And in portrait after portrait, as it were, year after year, one sees him getting thinner and more melancholy, his long fingers lost in his drooping cuffs, his coat hanging on his bony chest, an old man at thirty, eyes sunken, mouth set, face angular, only his wide brow, framed in the ringlets of a Louis XIV wig, unchanged.

Or let us look at his work: *Le Lorgneur* or *Le Flûteur* is Watteau himself. His negligent glance rests on the entwined couple whom he beguiles with his music. The silent musician accompanies their embraces, listens to their love-making, offering them serenades, untroubled, indifferent, and morose, besieged by boredom, like a professional musician at a wedding, tired of the dances he leads, and deaf to his singing violin . . .

Watteau personifies the modern artist in the finest and most disinterested sense of the word, the modern artist with his search for the ideal, his contempt for money, his lack of care for the morrow, his unplanned life — I nearly said his bohemian life but the word has become too discredited.

Edmond and Jules de Goncourt
on 'La Philosophie de Watteau' in *l'Artiste*, 1856
(Reprinted in *L'Art du Dix-huitième siècle*, 1859-75)

Notes on the illustrations

Frontispiece Boucher *Portrait of Watteau*. 8½ × 10 in. (21.5 × 25.3 cm.). Musée Condé, Chantilly.
A copy by Boucher of a self-portrait drawing by Watteau which is now lost. Boucher engraved this drawing and used it as a frontispiece to the *Figures de différents caractères*, a collection of engravings after a number of Watteau's drawings, published by Jean de Jullienne, between 1726 and 1728.

Figures 2 and 3 Rubens *Coronation of Marie de Medici*. 1622–25. 155⅜ × 300½ in. (3 m. 94 cm. × 7 m. 27 cm.), and *La Kermesse* 1635–38. 58⅝ × 103 in. (1 m. 49 cm. × 2 m. 61 cm.). Musée du Louvre, Paris.
The most important series of paintings by Rubens in Paris was the Medici cycle, executed between 1622 and 1625 for the Luxembourg Palace and now in the Louvre. Watteau had access to these when working for Claude III Audran and was particularly fascinated by the *Coronation of Marie de Medici*, although he seems to have concentrated on the detail of the dog in the foreground which reappears in many of his later works. The unbridled energy and richness of *La Kermesse*, then in the Royal Collection, also impressed him from an early date, as can be seen from the drawing he made of the couple embracing (plate 4).

Figures 4 and 5 Jacques Callot *Courtiers*. 3¼ × 2 in. (8 × 5 cm.).; 3 × 1½ in. (7.3 × 4.3 cm); 3¼ × 2 in. (8 × 5 cm.). Devonshire Collection, Chatsworth. *Soldiers*. 2¾ × 5¾ in (7 × 15 cm.). Musée du Louvre, Paris.
Jacques Callot (1592/3–1635) worked mainly in Nancy as an etcher of extraordinary imaginative power and technical precision. His subjects were taken from court life, from the theatre and from contemporary military manoeuvres. These drawings of courtiers and soldiers have a nervous elegance which obviously appealed to Watteau, who could have studied Callot's prints during his early years in Paris.

Figure 6 Claude Gillot *Scènes des deux Carrosses*. 52⅝ × 62¼ in. (134 × 158 cm.). Musée du Louvre, Paris.
One of the very few surviving paintings by Watteau's master, Claude Gillot, who is best remembered for his passion for all things theatrical and his inventiveness as a draughtsman. This is an extremely, almost oppressively literal record of an episode from Regnard's *La Foire Saint-Germain*, first performed at the Théâtre Italien in 1695. This particular scene, the comic climax of the play, was added after the first performance.

Figure 7 Claude III Audran *Singerie*. Red chalk, plumbago, and some wash. 28¾ × 21 in. (73.4 × 53.3 cm.). National-museum, Stockholm.
Design for a wall painting for the royal château of Marly, for which Audran received payment in 1709. The light cursive style of this kind of decoration brought a great deal of fresh air into French interiors in the early years of the eighteenth century. Audran, for whom Watteau worked as assistant in 1708 and 1709, was the great populariser of these arabesques, of which the inventor was the late seventeenth-century designer and engraver Jean I Bérain.

THE COLOUR PLATES

Plate 1 *Singerie*. Plumbago and red chalk. 27½ × 19½ in. (69.7 × 49.5 cm.). Nationalmuseum, Stockholm.
Sketch for a wall painting for the château of Marly, for which Watteau's master Claude III Audran was paid in 1709. An earlier, more schematic treatment of the composition, by Audran himself, is reproduced on page 14. This more advanced *singerie* (a caricatural drawing in which

humans are represented as apes) was for many years attributed to the master rather than the pupil; but although the composition is due to Audran, the infinitely more subtle and delicate handling reveals the technical gulf that yawns between the two men. Even at this very early date Watteau emerges as a draughtsman of genius, although as a painter his particular style takes longer to evolve.

Plate 2 *L'Enjôleur* (The Cajoler). Panel, 31¼ × 15⅜ in. (79.5 × 39 cm.). Cailleux Collection, Paris.
One of a series of eight decorative panels for a room in the Hôtel de Nointel (later Hôtel de Poulpry) in the rue de Lille, Paris, painted about 1708. Each panel consists of a single figure surrounded by an airy arabesque border which, although of standard design throughout the series, varies very slightly in treatment from panel to panel — a favourite Rococo conceit. The present example is unique in that it contains two figures, of vaguely theatrical mien; indeed, the spirit of pantomime is already omnipresent in this very early work and, in the form in which it manifests itself here, is clearly inspired by Gillot. Gillot rather than Audran is also the inspiration behind the conception of the arabesque; the design of four of the panels — *La Folie, Le Faune, Le Vendangeur* and *Bacchus* — can be compared with a drawing by Gillot in the Kaufman Collection in London.

Plate 3 *Le Faune.* Panel, 34¼ × 15⅜ in. (87 × 39 cm.). Cailleux Collection, Paris.
See note to *L'Enjôleur* (Plate 2).

Plate 4 *A couple, after Rubens.* Red chalk. 9¼ × 5¾ in. (23.3 × 14.7 cm.). Musée des Arts Décoratifs, Paris.
This couple appears in Rubens' picture *La Kermesse*, now in the Louvre. The drawing presumably dates from Watteau's association with Audran, who, in his capacity of curator of

the Luxembourg Palace, also had access to certain pictures in the royal collection. The couple in the drawing, although brawny, are treated with a certain tentative delicacy which would correspond with the date 1708–9.

Plate 5 *Le Pèlerin* (A Pilgrim). Red, black and white chalk on buff paper. 14⅝ × 9⅞ in. (37.2 × 25.1 cm.). Musée du Petit Palais, Paris.
Possibly intended for a series of engravings of single figures of street characters. A great number of such drawings were engraved after Watteau's death by Jean de Jullienne under the title, *Figures de différents caractères*. The delicacy of this drawing would indicate a date in the region of 1710. The man wears a scrip and a double rope of cockleshells (the pilgrim's emblem) and he carries a staff. The pilgrim theme preoccupied Watteau throughout his life, but in later works objectivity gave way to fantasy.

Plate 6 *Soldiers.* Red chalk. 7 × 8½ in. (17.4 × 21.8 cm.). École Nationale Supérieure des Beaux-Arts, Paris.
Connected with Watteau's military paintings and therefore datable 1709 or 1710. The figures in Watteau's early sketches have a miniature, stick-like elegance; here one sees the emergence of a broader, more incisive line.

Plate 7 *Le Défilé* (The March Past). 12¾ × 17 in. (32.4 × 43.2 cm.). City of York Art Gallery, York.
Although in poor condition and differing very slightly from the engraving by Moyreau, which is the only eighteenth-century evidence we have for its existence, apart from the title, this should be accepted as an authentic Watteau, painted in 1709 during his eight-month stay in Valenciennes. The decision to revert to the predominantly brown and Flemish character of his early manner while surrounded by the airily brilliant and sophisticated decorations of Audran would be

surprising if Watteau were not famous for his independence of taste. The military subjects, of which he painted perhaps a dozen, form a curious digression in the story of his development. Perhaps they represent a desire to escape from the blanket influence of Gillot and Audran, on whose decorative style it would have been difficult to improve. The present example reveals the strong influence of the Fleming, Van der Meulen, military painter to Louis XIV; it forms a pendant to *La Halte*, now believed to be in an American private collection.

Plate 8 *L'Accordée de Village* (The Village Bride). 25 ½ × 36 ¼ in. (63 × 92 cm.). Sir John Soane's Museum, London.
Connected stylistically with the military subjects of 1709–10 (this may be later): the final sophistication has not yet set in. The subject may have been suggested by Dancourt's comedy, *l'Opéra de Village*, of which the third act intermezzo is a village festival to celebrate a marriage contract. This theme was to be immensely successful throughout the first half of the eighteenth century; it was repeated endlessly by Watteau's pupils Lancret and Pater, and was carried to its ultimate point of exploitation by Greuze in 1761.

Plate 9 *L'Île de Cythère* (The Island of Cythera). 17 ¾ × 21 ¾ in. (46 × 55.5 cm.). Heugel Collection, Paris.
May be dated 1709 by virtue of the fact that Dancourt's play, *Les Trois Cousines*, of which this is an episode, was revived in that year. The scene represents the intermezzo at the end of Act III, in which 'Mlle Hortense, pèlerine' sings her famous song, inviting her companions to join the pilgrimage to the Isle of Love where they will find the husband or wife whom Venus has in store for them. As Watteau paints them, the characters are well within the tradition of musical comedy peasantry; very different from the fleshy worldly figures of the great picture of 1717, in which they appear to have grown older along with the painter. The simple disposition of the early picture, no doubt faithful to the actual disposition of the cast on the stage, was retained by Watteau in the later version, as were certain details of the clothing — for example, the cape of the woman with her back to the spectator. This picture represents Watteau's style before the great billow of Rubensian movement that was shortly to animate it.

Plate 10 *La Perspective*. 17 ¾ × 21 ½ in. (46.9 × 56.7 cm.). Museum of Fine Arts, Boston.
The architectural fragment has been identified as the portico of Pierre Crozat's country house at Montmorency, near Enghien, which enables us to date the picture from 1712–15, when Watteau was closely associated with Crozat and his various houses. In fact, this argument should not be carried too far, as Watteau was quite capable of storing up the memory for future reference. But the fact that this is primarily a landscape study, on which the figures have obviously been imposed, bears out the theory that this picture was painted at a definite time in a definite place. It therefore seems reasonable to suggest that the date may be 1714–15.

Plate 11 *Ceres* (Summer). 54 ½ × 49 ½ in. (138.5 × 125.8 cm.). National Gallery of Art, Washington, D.C. Samuel H. Kress Collection.
One of four oval paintings illustrating *The Seasons*, painted some time between 1712 and 1715 for the dining room of Pierre Crozat's town house in the rue de Richelieu, Paris. Opinion is now moving towards the conclusion that Watteau's association with Crozat did not become meaningful until 1715, although the commission must have been given and received before that date. *Spring*, recently rediscovered in a private collection in England, was destroyed by fire in May,

1966; *Autumn* and *Winter*, which are rather more ambitious and incorporate elements from Titian and Poussin, are known only from engravings. The unexpectedly large format and the generally blond tonality of the *Summer* may be due to the influence of Charles de la Fosse (see, for example, the latter's *Venus and Vulcan* in Nantes). La Fosse introduced Watteau to Crozat; an old tradition, now discredited, said that La Fosse supplied the original sketches for this series.

Plate 12 *L'Amour désarmé* (Love disarmed). 18½ × 15 in. (47 × 38 cm.). Musée Condé, Chantilly.
Inspired by a Veronese drawing which Watteau could have seen in the Crozat Collection. This picture is therefore contemporary with the *Seasons* and with the Louvre *Autumn*, although it lacks the delicate richness of the latter's colouring. Painted 1714–15.

Plate 13 *Jupiter and Antiope*. 28⅜ × 43¼ in. (72 × 110 cm.). Musée du Louvre, Paris.
When staying with Crozat Watteau is said to have made a particular study of Titian, Giacomo Bassano, Campagnola, Rubens and Van Dyck. This picture, with its contrast between the white flesh of the nymph and the brawny copper male nude, and its predominantly brown landscape with deep green-blue striations in the sky, reveals the determined Italianism of Watteau at this stage of his career. The phase was short-lived and is confined to the few nude and landscape studies made at this time. Painted about 1712–14.

Plate 14 *A Persian standing*. Red and black chalk. 9⅞ × 6¼ in. (25.1 × 15.7 cm.). Kunstverzamelingen, Teylers Stichting, Haarlem.
One of Watteau's few datable drawings. A Persian embassy, headed by Mohammed Riza Bey, visited Louis XIV at Versailles in 1715. Watteau made about ten drawings of various Persian personalities, which he may have intended to have engraved as none of them was incorporated into his paintings. On the back of this particular drawing there is a manuscript note by Caylus to the effect that the drawing was left to him by Watteau.

Plate 15 *Sirois and his Family* ('*Sous un habit de Mezzetin*'). 10⅜ × 7⅞ in. (26 × 20 cm.). Wallace Collection, London.
According to a manuscript note by Mariette, a portrait of Sirois and his family. Sirois, a picture dealer and ultimately father-in-law of Gersaint, was a good friend to Watteau, who lodged in his house on more than one occasion between 1710 and 1718. This picture is almost impossible to date with precision. The rococo, almost miniature, scale would seem to make it early, but the preliminary drawings in the British Museum and the Bordeaux-Groult Collection, Paris, have the broadness of handling of the mature period. The date 1716–18 is tentatively proposed.

Plate 16 *La Finette*. 10¼ × 7½ in. (25 × 19 cm.). Musée du Louvre, Paris.
Traditionally regarded as a pendant to *L'Indifférent* (plate 17). The figure seems to be a variation on an earlier *Polonaise*, now known only from an engraving, and is a far less precise characterisation than *L'Indifférent*. Rubbed almost to the point of no return, what was originally greenish satin shows slug trails of dirty white pigment.

Plate 17 *L'Indifférent*. 10⅜ × 8 in. (26 × 20 cm.). Musée du Louvre, Paris.
A portrait of an actor or dancer, very probably seen on stage. In a ruinous condition which gives it an air of convalescence; a drawing in the Museum Boymans Van Beuningen, Rotterdam, showing the figure in a similar pose but in reverse, is

on the contrary bursting with health. The masquerade costume could link this picture with various studies for the Louvre *Embarquement*, and it would probably be fair to date it about 1716.

Plate 18 *Two Studies of a Woman seated*. Red chalk. 8 × 13⅜ in. (20.2 × 34 cm.). Rijksmuseum, Amsterdam.
The figure on the left appears in *La Gamme d'Amour* (plate 19). Executed in about 1715–16.

Plate 19 *La Gamme d'Amour*. 20 × 23½ in. (50.8 × 58.4 cm.). National Gallery, London.
About 1715. This picture, which was apparently in a poor condition even before Watteau died, has something of the landscape mystery notable in *Assemblée dans un Parc* (plate 24). The two main figures recur in several other paintings by Watteau, notably the Berlin *Récréation galante*.

Plate 20 *Bal Champêtre* (*Les Plaisirs du Bal*). 19¾ × 24⅜ in. (50 × 62 cm.). Dulwich College Gallery, London.
Several versions of this picture exist, and doubts have been cast on the authenticity of the Dulwich picture. The packing of the figures on the extreme right and a certain lack of definition in the drawing might indicate a lesser hand than Watteau's to have been at work; on the other hand, the painting of the dresses of the two women with their backs to the spectator have all the hallmarks of Watteau's handling. The picture is usually dated 1719, but a certain confusion in the composition and a general over-accumulation of detail — in the landscape, for example — suggest less than Watteau's usual mastery. This may be an early essay in this type of multi-figure composition. The date 1714–15 is proposed.

Plate 21 *Harlequin and Columbine* (*Voulez-vous triompher des belles?*). 13½ × 10½ in. (34.3 × 25.7 cm.). Wallace Collection, London.
Larger in format and handling deeper in colour, more assured in spatial disposition than the *Sirois* (plate 15) with which it is often compared, this picture presents on a small scale many of the sophistications of Watteau's grander works, notably the impassive stone herm, the Van Dyckian supernumeraries, the astonishing modernity of the landscape fragment (the whole of Fragonard's future development may be forecast from here) and the succulent painting of the peach-coloured satin skirt which manages to reflect the red, blue and gold of Harlequin's costume. The masked Harlequin is such an uncompromisingly Italian figure that this picture might well date from the end of 1716, the date at which the Italian players returned to Paris.

Plate 22 *L'Amour au Théâtre Français*. 14½ × 18⅞ in. (37 × 48 cm.). Staatliche Museen, Gemäldegalerie Berlin-Dahlem.
This picture and its pendant, *L'Amour au Théâtre Italien* (see plate 23), might well have been inspired by the return of the Italian players to Paris in 1716, as the latter seems to reflect a precise theatrical impression. The titles need not be taken too seriously; both pictures represent groups of actors. The French example contains that mingling of noble and comic styles which Watteau will bring out much more forcibly in *Les Comédiens Francais*. Here, two actors appear to be half dressed in the allegorical costumes of Bacchus and Love, while on the extreme right the famous character player Paul Poisson appears as Crispin, the wily servant, a characterisation which he inherited from his father and which he made famous in plays like *Le Légataire universel* and *Les Folies amoureuses* by Jean-François Regnard. The female dancer and the bagpipe player will reappear in *Les Fêtes Vénitiennes* of about 1718.

Plate 23 *L'Amour au Théâtre Italien.* 14 ½ × 18 ⅞ in. (37 × 48 cm.). Staatliche Museen, Gemäldegalerie Berlin-Dahlem. For dating, see note to plate 22. This would seem to be a far more unified occasion than that depicted in *L'Amour au Théâtre Français*, which may simply indicate that Watteau was a more assiduous visitor to the Italian Comedy than to the Comédie Française. The French picture has a quality of fantasy and abstraction which is entirely absent here, as if Watteau had far less need to draw on his imagination when thoroughly captivated by the real thing. The main characters, reading from left to right, are Scaramouche, Isabella, Pierrot with his guitar, Harlequin (masked), Mezzetin with the candle, Pantalone and the Doctor. This composition, slightly rearranged, will be given sharper and more dramatic presentation in Dr Mead's picture of 1720, *Les Comédiens Italiens.*

Plate 24 *Assemblée dans un Parc.* 12 ⅝ × 18 ⅛ in. (32 × 46 cm.). Musée du Louvre, Paris.
Late 1716 or early 1717. This, like *Les Deux Cousines* (plate 25), might almost be considered as a first study for the Louvre *Embarquement*, although its powerful coppery romanticism has a more direct and less symbolic impact than the later work. The picture was painted in the first instance as a landscape study, and as such is one of Watteau's finest; the figures were added later with a more loaded brush. Watteau's disastrous habit of allowing his brushes to become clogged with oil is apparent in the slimed trails of pigment that describe the satin skirts. Nevertheless, the placing of these figures is marvellously sensitive; they sustain and intensify the mood of the landscape more brilliantly than any other exercise in this genre to date.

Plate 25 *Les Deux Cousines.* 12 × 14 in. (29 × 35 cm.). Marquis de Ganay Collection, Paris.

All three figures are standard favourites from Watteau's repertoire, but their juxtaposition is new. To the poignancy of being alone in the company of people who are obliviously together is added the poignancy of the landscape in the dying light of day. The theme and mood of the *Embarquement pour Cythère* (plate 27) are taking shape here. The standing girl almost fulfils the function of a piece of sculpture, and indeed she serves as echo and reflection to the two statues in the background. Here she adumbrates the symbolism of the term of Venus in the Louvre *Embarquement*. The date 1716 is proposed.

Plates 26 and 27 *L'Embarquement pour l'Île de Cythère* (The Embarkation for Cythera) and detail. 50 × 75 ½ in. (127 × 192 cm.). Musée du Louvre, Paris.
Painted in 1717 and presented to the Academy on August 28th of that year as *morceau de réception* under the title of *Pèlerinage à l'Île de Cythère*. As has been proved, this is more likely to be a return from the Isle of Love after the votive ceremonies have taken place: the dying light and the fact that the lovers are no longer single pilgrims but matched off in pairs would seem to substantiate this beyond future doubt. Like the greater number of Watteau's themes this was drawn from the theatre, quite specifically from an episode in Dancourt's *Les Trois Cousines*, first performed in Paris in 1700 and revived in 1709. An earlier version of the subject was *L'Île de Cythère* (Heugel collection, plate 9), an apparently literal reading of a scene from the play. Here Watteau has broadened the implications of the original episode until the result is something of his own creation. This is the most renowned of Watteau's pictures and in a sense the most philosophical. The device of narrating the essence of the action through the attitudes of the three main couples seated on the bluff (from right to left in this case) is a time-honoured one in the history of painting: a modern scholar has even compared

Watteau's method here with that used by Poussin in the *Israelites gathering Manna*.

Plate 28 *Study for L'Embarquement pour l'Île de Cythère*. Red, black and white chalks on buff paper. 13 ¼ × 8 ⅞ in. (33.6 × 22.6 cm.). British Museum, London.
One of the few drawings which Watteau made specifically for a painting — normally he composed his pictures from a selection of studies filed away in various albums. This drawing is therefore sketchier and less finished than his regular figure studies, and is rare in that Watteau is trying to solve a problem of movement and one which involves two people.

Plate 29 *L'Embarquement pour l'Île de Cythère*. 50 ¾ × 76 ¾ in. (130 × 192 cm.). Staatliche Museen, Gemäldegalerie Berlin-Dahlem.
A variant of the Louvre picture, painted for Jullienne. Something of the original pathos has been lost with the increase in the number of figures and the diminution of the impact of the landscape. There is also a loss of rigour in the transformation of Venus from a classic herm to a Rococo statuette and in the addition of a chorus of putti. In spirit we note a reversion from pilgrimage to masquerade. Nevertheless, the technical perfection of this bravura piece will leave its mark on eighteenth-century French painting, although only Fragonard will come near to emulating it in his *Fête à Saint-Cloud*.

Plate 30 *Three Studies of a Woman*. Black and red chalk and plumbago on buff paper. 9 × 11 ½ in. (23 × 29 cm.). Musée du Louvre, Paris.
One of the most pictorial of all Watteau's drawings, remarkable for the heavy chalking of the folds in the skirt and the extreme tension in the attitude of the woman on the left, who appears in *Les Charmes de la Vie* (plate 31). c. 1716.

Plate 31 *The Music Party (Les Charmes de la Vie)*. 25 ½ × 36 ¼ in. (64.8 × 92.1 cm.). Wallace Collection, London.
Usually dated about 1718 on the grounds that the figure on the extreme left has been identified as Vleughels, with whom Watteau shared a house in the rue du Cardinal Lemoine in 1718 and 1719. The compositional mastery would seem to substantiate this dating, although several details — notably the small Negro page, borrowed from Veronese's *Marriage at Cana*, and the dog borrowed from Rubens' *Coronation of Marie de Medici* — connect it with an earlier period of Watteau's life, about 1715–16. The setting, like that of the Dulwich *Plaisirs du Bal*, is the colonnade of the Tuileries, but the landscape has the character of a fantasy rather than a topographical view of the Champs-Elysées, as is usually stated. This is Watteau's most successful experiment in 'theatrical' space: the spectator occupies a position analogous to the front row of the stalls, and the pavement is equivalent to the ramp of a stage. There are signs that Watteau is relying less on his habit of using drawings from his sketchbook than usual: the dog, for example, is much too large in scale, as is the page. A more purely painterly approach emerges in the silhouetting of the main figure against the broadly painted middle distance. The perfection of the clover-pink satin costume of the musician cannot be over-emphasised.

Plate 32 *Study of a Negro*. Red and black chalk heightened with white on grey paper. 7 ⅛ × 5 ¾ in. (18 × 14.5 cm.). British Museum, London.
A broad and beautiful study, worthy of Van Dyck. This is one of a number of drawings of a Negro model who appears in *Les Charmes de la Vie* (plate 31). Executed in about 1716–17.

Plate 33 *The Concert*. 26 × 35 ¾ in. (66 × 91 cm.). Verwaltung der Staatlichen Schlösser und Gärten, Charlottenburg-Berlin.

A variant of *Les Charmes de la Vie* in the Wallace Collection, although apart from the central motif of musician, child and guitar, the two compositions are entirely different. The Potsdam picture must certainly be earlier; the landscape has the visionary character associated with the Louvre *Embarquement* while a similar dreaminess becalms the figures. Painted late 1716 or early 1717.

Plate 34 *Two Studies of a Bagpipe Player*. Red chalk with touches of black and white chalk. 11 × 8¼ in. (28 × 21 cm.). Musée du Louvre, Paris.
A man playing the bagpipe figures in many of Watteau's works, ranging from the early *Accordée de Village* (plate 8) to the comparatively late *Fêtes Vénitiennes* (plate 35). The model was probably the actor La Thorillière. This particular drawing may date from about 1716.

Plate 35 *Les Fêtes Vénitiennes*. 21½ × 17¾ in. (54.5 × 45 cm.). National Gallery of Scotland, Edinburgh.
About 1718. The figure on the left has been identified as Vleughels, the Flemish painter with whom Watteau shared a house in the rue du Cardinal Lemoine in 1718 and 1719. His costume may be connected with the drawings made by Watteau in 1715 on the occasion of the visit of the Persian embassy of Mohammed Riza Bey to the court of Versailles. The subject of the picture was probably suggested by the minuet intermezzo in the ballet, *Les Fêtes Vénitiennes*, first performed at the Paris Opéra in 1710 and retained in the repertory until about 1740. This is one of Watteau's most important pictures: the landscape and atmospheric mastery of the *Embarquement* are allied to the first signs of the wry realism notable in Watteau's latest works.

Plate 36 *Nude Woman*. Red, black and white chalks. 9¹/₁₆ × 9¹/₁₆ in. (23 × 23 cm.). Musée des Beaux-Arts, Lille.

This beautiful and bulky drawing displays all the broadness of Watteau's later works and was perhaps executed in about 1719. Certain of the black chalk strokes appear to be later additions.

Plate 37 *Le Mezzetin*. 21 × 16¾ in. (53.5 × 42.5 cm.). Metropolitan Museum of Art, New York, Munsey Fund, 1934.
Occasionally described as a portrait of Angelo Constantini, the most famous Mezzetino of his day, this marvellous picture is more likely to be a *portrait imaginaire*. The statue, with her back to the singer, is an allusion to the ardour and also the hopelessness of the serenade. The strenuous attitude of the singer's head, however, denotes a certain irony which underlines Watteau's loyalty to the values of the pantomime rather than his sympathy with the undertaking. This can probably be dated 1718–19.

Plates 38 and 39 *Les Champs Elysées* and detail. 12½ × 16⅜ in. (31.4 × 40.6 cm.). Wallace Collection, London.
About 1718–19. A rather tired painting, with a certain carelessness of handling: parallel hatchings for grass in the passage separating the foreground from the background groups, slug trails of dirty pigment in the satin dresses, features not modelled but indicated by flecks of dark paint. Embedded in the midst of this rather listless tract of canvas is a miniature landscape of marvellous freshness which must have been painted *sur le motif*. Here again we get an indication that towards the end of his life Watteau's method of painting — from existing studies — was breaking down and giving way to a more direct approach to his subject.

The statue is a variation of the Louvre *Antiope* (see plate 13).

Plate 40 *Fête in a Park*. 49 × 74 in. (125 × 188 cm.). Wallace Collection, London.

A larger, weaker, variation of *Les Champs Elysées* (see plate 39). The main changes are in scale, in the substitution of a man for a woman on the left of the main group, the addition of a group of playing children on the left and of a group and several figures in the middle distance. The sculpture of the sleeping nymph has been replaced by one of a livelier, more Baroque figure which appears in other works by Watteau. A late work, very similar to *Le Rendez-vous de Chasse* (plate 41); about 1720–21.

This is an interesting example of an essentially small composition blown up to excessive scale, and shows Watteau's new interest in attacking a large canvas. He has not been very successful here: the mechanical handling of the foreground foliage in particular shows that the demands of the new format are not fully understood.

Plate 41 *Le Rendez-vous de Chasse* (The Halt during the Chase). 48½ × 74 in. (124 × 187 cm.). Wallace Collection, London.
This work is referred to in a letter to Julienne written on September 2nd, 1720.

At the end of his life Watteau obviously found it unsatisfactory for one reason or another, to work on the fine figure scale of his earlier years. Here is an enormous canvas, the same size as the *Fête in a Park* (plate 40) but much more successfully handled. The perspective is broader, the multiplicity of small groups has gone, even the problem of filling the foreground is on the verge of being resolved. The figures silhouetted against the middle distance have the painterly quality characteristic of these last years.

Plate 42 *La Toilette*. 17½ × 14¼ in. (44 × 37 cm.). Wallace Collection, London.
The date 1720 is proposed in view of the following facts: the blander texture and slacker forms, the broader, more

painterly brushwork, the decreased dependence on drawing, the strong vein of realism, all of which can be seen in other works of this period, such as *The Italian Players* (plate 46), *Gilles* (plate 47), and *Le Rendez-vous de Chasse* (plate 41). The closer attention to genre details, such as the maidservant's cap, may have been inspired by Philippe Mercier, whom Watteau knew in England. This picture had a considerable influence on Boucher and Fragonard, particularly the latter, and is also the source of many typical eighteenth century studies on this theme.

Plate 43 *The Judgement of Paris*. 18½ × 12¼ in. (47 × 31 cm.). Musée du Louvre, Paris.
Traditionally called a late work, although difficult to categorise owing to the extreme and uncharacteristic pearliness of the paint. Possibly a sketch made for one of the pictures in the background of *L'Enseigne de Gersaint*, although it does not appear in that work. Nevertheless, both the composition and the handling would seem to connect it with this project; datable, therefore, in the spring of 1721.

Plate 44 *L'Enseigne de Gersaint*. 71¾ × 121¼ in. (182 × 307 cm.). Staatliche Museen, Gemäldegalerie Berlin-Dahlem.
Painted at Watteau's own request as a shop sign for his friend Edmé Gersaint's picture gallery, 'A l'Enseigne du Grand Monarque', Pont Notre Dame, in the spring of 1721. Gersaint says that it was completed in eight days. In view of its size it seems likely that the *Enseigne* formed part of the façade of the shop and that one looked up to it from below. It was *in situ* for only fifteen days before being bought by M. Claude Glucq. The picture was divided into two parts some time in the middle of the eighteenth century when it was already in the Prussian royal collection.

The scale of the canvas and the realism of the detail

correspond with other realist masterpieces of Watteau's last years. One may also note a tendency towards a more rigorously centrifugal type of composition, notable in the *Italian Players*, the *Gilles*, and, supremely, here. It is, in fact, the compositional problem which seems to have been Watteau's major preoccupation in the *Enseigne*. The new genre interest seen in *La Toilette* reappears in the figures of the packers and the *vendeuse*; the customers, whose gestures have been adumbrated in many *fêtes galantes*, are brought into sharper focus by virtue of having precise functions to perform. No adequate study has been made of the pictures on the walls. Are they a personal selection or the actual stock? The portraits look Dutch or Spanish, and of the large compositions one can just distinguish a *Pan and Syrinx*, an *Ecstasy of St. Benedict*, a *Silenus*, a *Sleeping Nymph*, a *Mystic Marriage of St Catherine* and two pictures in the genre of Watteau himself (between the heads of the man and woman on the left and just above the large oval painting on the right), although they do not correspond to known compositions. (Owing to the intrusion of mouldings on the Rococo frame into the picture itself, a small area has had to be removed from the four sides of the reproduction.)

Plate 45 *Les Comédiens Français*. 22½ × 28¾ in. (57 × 33 cm.). Metropolitan Museum of Art, New York, Jules S. Bache Collection, 1949.
Painted in 1720 as pendant to *Les Comédiens Italiens* (plate 46). As in the latter, the three main characters can be easily identified as Mlle Duclos, M. Beaubourg and, mounting the stairs, M. Poisson. Elements of tragedy and comedy are combined to give a succinct impression of the state of the French theatre in 1720. The costumes here are no less traditional than those of the Italian players: Poisson was faithful to his sixteenth century Spanish outfit, while later in the century Noverre speaks of the quantities of silver lace to which the French actors were so deeply attached. The palace setting and the rhetorical gestures were also obligatory.

Plate 46 *Les Comédiens Italiens* (The Italian Players). 26½ × 31⅞ in. (67.5 × 81 cm.). National Gallery of Art, Washington D.C. Samuel H. Kress Collection.
Painted in London in 1720 for Dr Mead. The cast has been identified as the company of Luigi Riccoboni, known as Lelio, who brought the Italian Comedy back to Paris in 1716 after a period of banishment which had lasted for nineteen years. An intensely theatrical picture, in which many of the characters familiar from Watteau's earlier works seem to have found their true identity and in so doing have shed a dimension of mystery. This astonishing reversion from the general to the particular shows how brisk and rapid Watteau's method had become in his last years; very few drawings are known for the late works, and this absence of detailed preliminary studies is discernible in the increased slackness of the forms. At the same time the repertory of gesture and expression is increased.

Plate 47 *Gilles*. 72⅜ × 58⅝ in. (184 × 149 cm.). Musée du Louvre, Paris.
A very late work, an enlargement and development of the central figure in Dr Mead's *Italian Players* of 1720; probably 1721. Almost certainly intended as a theatre signboard, as the subject was a popular theatrical sketch of the time. The treatment is very broad and the painting was obviously meant to be seen from a distance: the white satin trousers and coral ribbons on the shoes show none of Watteau's usual bravura handling, but the effect is brilliantly convincing.

1

2

5

6

7

8

13

14

15

16

18

19

22

23

24

28

29

30

34

37

38

40

41

43

45

46

cuillère
kweeáir

verre
d'eau
vayr do

crêpe
krep

6
six seece

7
sept set

glace
glass

pomme
pom

8
huit weet

9
neuf nurf

croissant
krwassón

avion
aveeón

dix deece

Toto in France

BIDDY STREVENS

A first taste of France and the French language

PASSPORT BOOKS
a division of *NTC Publishing Group*
Lincolnwood, Illinois USA

For Thomas and all his friends

This edition first published in 1992 by Passport Books, a division
of NTC Publishing Group.
4255 West Touhy Avenue, Lincolnwood (Chicago), Illinois 60646-1975 U.S.A.

Originally published by Little, Brown and Company (UK) Limited.

Illustrations and text © 1992 by Bridget Strevens Romer.

Library of Congress Catalogue Number 91-066426

Toto and his parents have just arrived in Paris.

"I'll take you up to Sylvie's apartment. Hurry up now! Our taxi is waiting."
Toto's father presses the button on the intercom.

"Have a great day!" says Toto's mother, giving him a big hug.

"*Bonjour, Messieurs!*" says a lady cleaning the floor.
"Go on Toto, say '*Bonjour Madame*' to the *concierge*!" Toto's father insists.
"*Excusez-moi!* That's all the French I know." Toto replies, climbing the stairs.
"Are we almost there? Will you carry my plane, Dad?"

"Fourth floor on the right. Here we are at last!" says Toto's father.

"May I ring the bell?" Toto asks.

"*Bonjour* Toto!" says Sylvie, kissing him on each cheek. Paulette kisses him twice too.

"Woof!" says Mimi in dog language.

"See you later, Toto!" Toto's father waves at them.

"*A bientôt!*"

"Come and have breakfast!" says Sylvie, sitting down at the table, "*du pain* – just the way I like it!" Sylvie dunks some bread into her *chocolat chaud*.

"Wow, I've never seen such a big bowl of hot chocolate!" Toto whistles, "and a *croissant* and jam, yummy!"

"Oh no! Paulette, look what Mimi's doing!"

Now Mimi can't speak French *or*
English, but you can tell she wants to
go out for a walk.

"Wait for us Mimi!" they all shout
as she races down the stairs and out into
the street.

"*Vite, vite!* Hurry! Come back Mimi!" they all cry as she runs into the busy boulevard. "Stop that dog!"

Mimi runs twice around a hot-chestnut stand and through the legs of a man sweeping the street.

"*Ça, alors!*" he says, which simply means "Well, I never!"

"*Excusez-moi!*" Toto interrupts a man making pancakes. "Did you see a dog run past here?"

"*Oui, par là!* That way!" the man points.

"*Aie, aie, aie,*" Sylvie wails, "I've got a stitch from running too fast!"

Outside a pet shop Mimi suddenly screeches to a halt. What is this? Someone is standing on her leash!

"*Un chien! Ça alors!*" the pet shop owner says to himself. "My lucky day!"

"*Ça alors!*" cries a parrot peering over his shoulder.

"Mimi can't be far now," Toto thinks to himself.

"*Excusez-moi!*" he speaks to a man standing on one leg outside a pet shop.
"Did you see a dog run past here?"

"*Un chien? Non!*" The man shakes his head slowly. But then he points and says
"...*Ah, oui. Par là!*"

Toto has no idea what the man is doing with his other leg. Mimi finds herself in
a cage with some white mice. Poor Mimi! She doesn't know what to say to them.
She can't speak Mouse.

"What a beautiful dog! André, wait!" a lady orders her *chauffeur*.

"Aren't you cute!" she tells Mimi.

"That's funny," says the pet-shop owner, "you look just like that singer, what's-her-name . . . Sophie Starlette."

"But I AM Sophie Starlette," the lady says proudly. "Now tell me, *Monsieur*, how much is that dog?"

"*Ce chien, Madame?* Very special," he sniffs, "very expensive, but worth every *centime*. Ten thousand francs!"

By lunchtime, Toto, Sylvie, and Paulette are halfway up the *Avenue de l'Opéra*.

"It's no use looking any more! We've lost her forever!" Paulette bursts into tears.

"Where can you be, Mimi? Please come back, wherever you are. I miss you already," Sylvie whispers to herself.

"Don't worry. I'm sure we'll find her somehow," Toto comforts them.

Mimi looks around. Something tells her nose that her old friends are nearby. The traffic light turns red – and off she goes!

"*Mon chien, au secours*, help!" Sophie Starlette shouts, waving her arms.

"Mimi, you're back!" Paulette cries, "It's a miracle!"

Mimi licks everyone on both cheeks and wags her tail.

"But what happened? How did you get here?" Toto wonders.

"That's MY dog. I bought it this morning!" cries Sophie Starlette. What a commotion! Everyone is shouting and waving their arms.

"It's a SHE!" "She belongs to US!" reply Sylvie and Toto.

"Woof! Woof!" replies Mimi.

"*S'il vous plaît,*" a *gendarme* appears and raises his hands.

"IF YOU PLEASE, ONE story at a time! . . .

. . . What does the dog have to say for itself?"

"Look!" Toto points. "She wants us to follow her!"

Toto holds Mimi's leash as tightly as he can and sets off with a line of very disgruntled people following behind.

"But this is where I bought my dog this morning!" cries Sophie Starlette, ". . . and that's the man who sold him to me!"

"He's running away! Quick, let's get him, Mimi!" Toto shouts. All the pets start squeaking, mewing, barking, whistling and cawing in a hundred and one different languages. "*Par là, par là,*" the parrot screeches.

"After him, Mimi, *vite, vite!*" Toto shouts.

"*Attention!*" a fruit seller cries out. "Watch where you're going!"

Too late, there are apples all over the place.

"*Excusez-moi!*" Toto calls back though it's not his fault.

Suddenly the villain disappears into a shop.

The *boulangerie* is full of the delicious smell of freshly baked bread, but Mimi smells a rat! She pulls toward the counter.

"There, behind the *croissants*!" Toto shouts.

"I arrest you in the name of the law!" the *gendarme* declares as he grabs hold of the villain. He quickly takes him away in handcuffs.

"André, take a picture of us all!" Sophie Starlette orders her *chauffeur*. She kisses everyone on each cheek.

"Darling Mimi, thanks to you I won't feel so lonely. You must come and visit me, with all your friends. We'll go out for some wonderful walks together, won't we?"

"Oh, please don't talk about walking!" groans Sylvie. "*J'ai faim!*"

"I'm starving too!" says Toto. "Woof, WOOF!" Mimi agrees.

"We didn't have lunch!" Paulette explains.

"No lunch?" cries Sophie. "Well then, let me take you all to a *café* for a big treat!"

"*Bon appétit!*" says Sophie. And she orders them huge *sandwiches mixtes*, followed by *petits pains au chocolat* and *tartes aux pommes*.

The *garçon* then brings them a final treat.

"*Une glace à la fraise! Merci beaucoup!*" says Sylvie.

"Thank you . . ." says Toto. "*Merci!* Strawberry ice cream – my favorite! This drink is yummy too."

"It's called *grenadine*," Sophie tells him, "but I like *jus d'orange* better."

"*De l'eau, s'il vous plaît!*" Paulette asks for more water for Mimi, who is very thirsty and hungry after all that running.

Sophie Starlette then gives them cassettes of her songs and a picture of them all. Finally, she takes them home in her big car.

"*A bientôt!*" she waves good-bye. "See you soon!"

Now it's eight o'clock and time for *le dîner*.
 "I couldn't eat another thing," says Toto wearily.

It's very late when mom and dad arrive to take Toto back with them to the *hôtel*.
 "*Bonne nuit, Paulette. Merci! Au revoir!*"

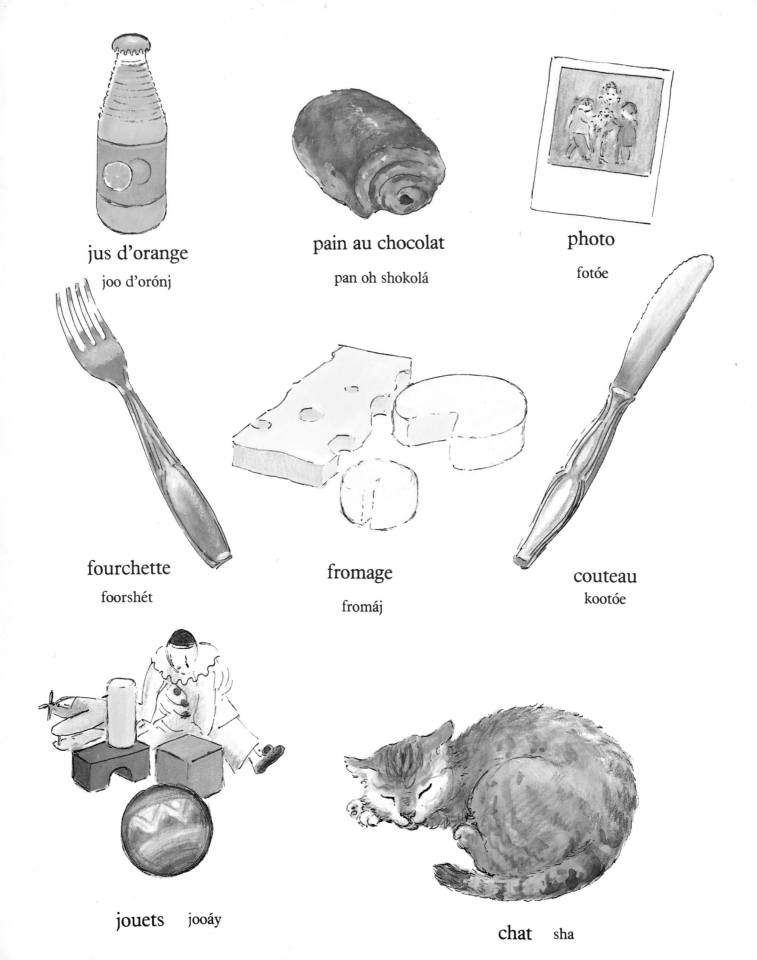

jus d'orange

joo d'orónj

pain au chocolat

pan oh shokolá

photo

fotóe

fourchette

foorshét

fromage

fromáj

couteau

kootóe

jouets   jooáy

chat   sha